for
Freedom

for Freedom

THE STORY OF A FRENCH SPY

KIMBERLY BRUBAKER BRADLEY

DELACORTE PRESS

Published by
Delacorte Press
an imprint of
Random House Children's Books
a division of Random House, Inc.
New York

Visit us on the Web! www.randomhouse.com/kids
Educators and librarians, for a variety of teaching tools, visit us at
www.randomhouse.com/teachers

Library of Congress Cataloging-in-Publication Data
Bradley, Kimberly Brubaker.
  For freedom : the story of a French spy / Kimberly Brubaker Bradley.
      p. cm.
Summary: Despite the horrors of World War II, a French teenager pursues her dream of
becoming an opera singer, which takes her to places where she gains information about
what the Nazis are doing—information that the French Resistance needs.
  ISBN 0-385-72961-8 (trade) — ISBN 0-385-90087-2 (GLB)
  1. World War, 1939–1945—France—Juvenile fiction. 2. France—History—German
occupation, 1940–1945—Juvenile fiction. [1. World War, 1939–1945—France—Fiction.
2. World War, 1939–1945—Underground movements—France—Fiction. 3. Singing—
Fiction. 4. Spies—Fiction. 5. France—History—German occupation, 1940–1945—
Fiction.] I. Title.
  PZ7.B7247 Fo 2003
  [Fic]—dc21   2002013057

The text of this book is set in 12-point Galliard.
Book design by Trish Parcell Watts
Printed in the United States of America
May 2003
10 9 8 7 6 5
BVG

This book is written as fiction
but tells a true story.

Suzanne David Hall,
former opera singer and spy for France,
graciously shared her stories with me.

I dedicate this book to Suzanne
and her husband, Larson,
and to their family,
with thanks.

CHAPTER ONE

*F*or me the war began on May 29, 1940. I was thirteen years old.

It was a Wednesday, the day we studied catechism and had choir practice and then had the afternoon free. Of course, I had to remain after choir to rehearse my solo, but when that was finished I found my friend Yvette. Together we went to Soeur Margritte.

"*S'il vous plaît,* please, Soeur Margritte, may we go down to the beach?" we asked.

Our convent school was high among the hills of Cherbourg; school was farther from the beach than my own home. But while we were not permitted home except on weekends, we were sometimes permitted to go about town. Yvette and I were good students, well behaved. *Always follow the rules,* my papa told me, *and you will be all right.* I always did, and I always was.

"We will take our homework," Yvette said.

"It's such a beautiful day," I said.

"We will be back before supper," we chorused.

France had been at war with Germany for nearly six months, yet there had been so little fighting that it seemed to mean nothing. The German army had spread across Europe, almost unopposed; neither the French nor the British had done much to stop them. There were English soldiers stationed in Cherbourg—I saw them when Maman and I went to the market on Saturdays—but they were quiet and polite and never bothered anyone. I couldn't imagine them actually fighting. Some days it was hard to believe we were in a real war.

Which is not to say we weren't paying attention. We listened to the radio and read the newspaper reports with increasing dread. We knew Hitler was coming; we feared that nothing could stop him. Papa and Maman talked in low voices at the dinner table, and sometimes Papa pounded his fist on the table and swore. "That Hitler!" he would say. "That cursed son of Satan!"

But I was only thirteen. My brothers, Pierre and Etienne, were fourteen and sixteen, too young to be soldiers; Etienne was lame as well. And I was studying to be a famous opera singer. I loved singing like nothing else. At Christmas I had sung a solo in the church choir, Gounod's "Ave Maria," and our director had said I was talented and should pursue a career. So now I had a music tutor, Madame Marcelle; I took special voice lessons twice a week and practiced hard every day.

So it was not that I was not paying attention to the war, but that I never thought the war could hurt me.

"Yes," Soeur Margritte decided. She was the nicest of the sisters. "It's a beautiful day, and who knows how many carefree days we have left. You may go. Have a nice time—but do your homework!"

We skipped down the cobblestone streets. The wind blowing in from the Channel tousled our skirts, pulled at our hair. I sang an aria from *Carmen* as we drew closer. *Carmen* was my favorite opera. I knew most of the part of Carmen, but I still could not reach some of the high notes.

"Oh, *tais-toi*," said Yvette, rolling her eyes at me. "Be quiet. Singing, always singing. I bet you sing in your sleep."

I probably did sing in my sleep. Someday I would sing in Paris. I dreamed of it all the time. "I'll ask Odette," I said. Odette was one of my roommates. I hummed a few notes, then began again. "*Ah! je t'aime, Escamillo, je t'aime, et que je meure si j'ai jamais aimé quelqu'un autant que toi!* Ah, I love you, Escamillo, I love you, and may I die if I have ever loved anyone as much as you!"

Yvette grinned. "What a horrible song!" She tossed her hair over her shoulder, flung her arm out dramatically, and began to sing, "*Savez-vous planter les choux? Do you know how to plant cabbages?*" A simple nursery song. Her voice wobbled, up, down, down, up.

Singing is a talent. You have it or you don't.

"Come on!" I said, running toward the sea.

We went to the Place Napoléon, the big square near the Gare Maritime, the station where trains could pull right up to the harbor to load and unload the ships. The Church of La Trinité formed part of the square, and from the benches around the edge we could watch the ships in the harbor, the waves curling, and the birds wheeling overhead. People strolled back and forth across the square.

We settled onto a bench in the sun. I opened my history book. History was my favorite subject. Yvette sniffed the air as though it were a flower. "It's so nice to be outside," she said, "after being stuck in that stuffy school all day. You're not going to start with the books already, are you? Let's talk."

"Okay." I closed my book and looked around. "The harbor's empty. That's odd." Cherbourg had an important harbor; before the war big ships had come often. I had been on the *Queen Elizabeth* once, when she was docked at Cherbourg.

Yvette looked too. "Not really," she said. "It's such a pretty day. If I had a boat, I'd take it out today too."

"*Bonjour,* Yvette," came a woman's pleasant voice. "*Bonjour,* Suzanne."

"*Bonjour, madame,*" we said. Our friend Madame Montagne waved to us as she came nearer. Her little son, Simon, skipped down to the water's edge and threw rocks into the waves. The Montagnes lived near Yvette's family, and Madame Montagne was Yvette's mother's friend. Since I was Yvette's best friend, I had known Madame Montagne for years.

"Where's Marie?" I asked. Marie was her daughter, two years old, a beautiful child with wide blue eyes.

"With her grandmother," Madame Montagne said. She patted her bulging belly happily. She was going to have a baby very soon; we often talked to her about it. Yvette was knitting her a pair of tiny booties. "I have grown too fat and I can't carry her this far. But Simon wanted to walk down to the beach. It's such a pretty day." She looked up. "Is that a plane?"

There was a far-off buzzing noise. It did sound like a plane.

"*Salut,* Simon!" Yvette yelled. Simon waved to her.

I hummed a scale to myself, D minor, as I found my place in my history book again.

The buzzing noise grew louder.

"Simon!" called Madame Montagne. "Do not get your shoes wet! Stay out of the water!" She started to walk toward him.

Suddenly the noise turned into a roar. Planes swarmed overhead, many of them, their engines fast and loud.

I jumped to my feet. My books slid to the ground. Yvette turned toward me, her eyes wide. She said something I didn't hear.

The beach, the square, exploded.

A bomb landed directly in front of us, throwing up a huge spray of fire and rock, making a noise louder than anything I had ever heard. I threw myself to the ground. Yvette dropped beside me, and we cowered beneath the bench, our arms over our heads. Bomb after bomb fell around us. I think I screamed, but I couldn't hear myself in the noise.

Then the planes flew on. There was a moment of near-silence, broken immediately by screams. On the hills of the city I could see smoke where fires burned. A siren began to wail.

Giant holes pockmarked the Place Napoléon. Not too far from us lay a body, a spreading pool of blood darkening the ground around it. *"Madame!"* screamed Yvette. We ran.

She was dead, torn apart. Her stomach had been ripped open. Beside her lay her little baby, never born but dead now too. A little girl, all covered in blood.

Yvette was screaming something, and now I caught the words: "She has no head! She has no head!"

I had been looking at the baby. I looked where Madame Montagne's head should have been, and then I took my sweater off and dropped it over that spot. Yvette shook like a sapling in a storm, screaming and crying and trembling all at the same time. I took her sweater and used it to cover the tiny baby.

Yvette backed up, still shaking, and turned on her heel as if to run. I whipped around and caught her hard by the arm. "We stay," I said, holding her tightly. "We stay here with Madame Montagne."

I didn't see little Simon anywhere, though I searched and searched with my eyes. There were craters, rubble; he could be anywhere. *Please, God, let him have run home*, I prayed. *Please, God, let him live.*

Our sweaters were deep blue, so they only darkened a little as Madame Montagne's blood soaked them. The cold wind whipped through our thin dresses. Blood ran down my arms and legs from narrow deep cuts that covered me. When it began to dry, my skin grew sticky. The flags flying near the church snapped on their poles. All around us, sirens screamed. Seabirds cried until I could hardly distinguish one noise from another.

Yvette had a gash on her cheek. Her white kneesocks were splattered red and brown. I could feel how mine stuck to me.

Yvette shook and sobbed. I shook, but not as much. She vomited. I did not, though I could feel my insides twisting and had to clench my teeth hard.

Eventually an ambulance came for Madame Montagne. I started to walk toward the ocean, to look for Simon, but Yvette collapsed the moment I let go of her arm. I went back to her and hauled her to her feet. "There was a little boy," I told the ambulance driver. "A boy, here. Simon Montagne." The driver nodded and said something to me, but I couldn't understand him for the ringing in my ears. Yvette moaned and her legs gave way. I hauled her up again. "Come," I said. "Come. Walk."

In a daze we staggered back to school. Yvette stumbled, and I held her up. Once I could not hold her and we both fell. I skinned my knees against the cobblestones.

"Walk," I said. *"Walk."* The convent would be safe. The sisters would know what to do.

As we approached the gate, Soeur Margritte ran to meet us. "Oh, *mon Dieu*," she cried. Her voice sounded like a seagull's cry, thin and wailing. "Oh, God in heaven. What happened? What should we do?"

Soeur Margritte was supposed to tell me what to do. "There were planes," I said. "Bombs. Madame Montagne—" Yvette cried out and crumpled to the ground, her hands over her face. Soeur Margritte huddled over her.

A flock of people, sisters and students, rushed out the doors and surrounded us. Soeur Marie-Auguste, the principal, took me gently by the arm. "Suzanne? Are you much hurt?"

I shook my head.

"Come," she said very gently, as though speaking to a tiny child. "Come with me. I will take you home." She led me away. I looked over my shoulder, wondering what was happening to Yvette.

⌒ハ

Maman cried out in horror when she saw me, and rushed to put her arms around me.

"I'm not really hurt," I said.

Maman pulled back to look at me. "You are bleeding. You're covered in blood."

"We went to the square. Madame Montagne—and Yvette—it was so loud. Simon's lost, I couldn't find him, there were bombs—" I couldn't stop my teeth from chattering, couldn't find enough words to tell the story.

"Shhh," Maman said. "Don't talk. Try not to think about it." She sat me down on a kitchen chair, and she telephoned Dr. Leclerc and then my father. Dr. Leclerc lived just down the street from us, but Papa arrived first. He hugged me hard. It hurt; I had little sharp pieces of something embedded in my arms. I flinched, and he stepped back. He looked furious. I couldn't tell whether he was angry at me or at the school.

"That Hitler," he said at last. "That son of Satan."

So he was not angry at me or the school.

My brothers were at their school, the monastery school for boys. I prayed they were safe. Surely we would have heard by now if their school had been hit. I wondered where they had been when the bombs fell, whether they had heard them, what they had done. I wondered how they would react when they learned about Madame Montagne. Did they know this was possible in Cherbourg? Was I the only one surprised?

Dr. Leclerc came and examined my wounds. I had splinters of sharp rock and metal all through my lower arms, and some in my legs as well. Shrapnel, it was called. Dr. Leclerc carefully picked out as much of it as he could. He washed the cuts and bandaged my arms loosely. My arms had felt numb after the bombing, but now they hurt as if they were on fire. "Some of the shrapnel is still deeply embedded," he said. "It will work its way to the surface of your skin in time. Or not. Perhaps you will always carry it with you."

"I want to carry nothing from this day with me." My words came out stiff and angry.

"So? You are not one who cries, eh?" Dr. Leclerc patted my cheek with approval. He lived three doors down from us. His office was the lower part of his house. I had known him and his wife and his two little children forever. "Tough girl."

What good would crying do?

"Madame Montagne is dead," I said. "We could not find her son, Simon."

Dr. Leclerc nodded. "I will pray for her," he said, "and I'll try to find out about Simon. If I learn anything, I'll let you know."

Maman made me tea and warmed some soup for my supper. She sat beside me while I sipped half a bowl. My teeth chattered against the spoon. My stomach closed against the soup.

"Never mind," Maman said. She led me upstairs and helped me into my nightgown. "Shall I sit with you until you're asleep?"

"Yes, please," I whispered.

I had not said much about what had happened. I tried not to think about it, but in honesty I could think of nothing else; Maman and I waited together in the dark for a long time before sleep came. When I did sleep, I dreamed of the screech of the bombs. Madame Montagne was screaming, and Yvette spun away from me as bombs exploded between us. I jerked awake. Maman was gone. The pain in my arms made it difficult to sleep again.

CHAPTER TWO

The next morning I returned to school. Maman wanted me to stay home. I knew the sisters would have understood if I had, but I felt compelled to go despite the blood seeping through the bandages on my arms. I didn't want to let the war affect me. I didn't want to give up so much as one day of school. "I must go," I said. "Yvette will need me. I must."

Maman looked at Papa, and Papa shrugged. "Let her go," he said. "The doctor didn't say to keep her home. Let her be with her friends."

So Maman walked me back to school. She stayed with me for morning Mass. "I don't see Yvette," I whispered when we were kneeling after Communion. "Where do you think she is?"

Maman shook her head. I decided Yvette must be somewhere behind me, where it was hardest to look without angering the sisters. Then when Mass was over and I still couldn't find her, I decided she must have slept late. Surely when she woke she would come.

One class passed, then another. I barely heard the words the sisters spoke. Yvette didn't come. All day long I looked for her.

What if she was hurt? I didn't think her wounds had been worse than mine, but what if I was wrong? Why hadn't I checked on her the night before? Yvette was the one person who completely understood me; she was funny and gentle, and ever since we were small she had been my best friend. I had never been homesick at boarding school, because Yvette was there. I depended on her.

"Soeur Elisabeth," I said to my etiquette teacher at the end of the day, "where's Yvette?"

Soeur Elisabeth was not a smiling sort of person. She looked especially harsh now. "Yvette's mother sent a note," she said. "She will come back when she is able."

"What's wrong with her?" I asked. "Was she hurt?" *I shouldn't have made her walk so far,* I thought. *I should have taken her home or made her get into the ambulance.*

Soeur Elisabeth hesitated. "I think she isn't hurt in her body," she said finally, "but it must have been dreadful yesterday, the things you saw."

I had been able to get through school only by blocking the previous day completely from my mind. I didn't reply to Soeur Elisabeth. I could think of nothing to say.

"Pray for Yvette," said Soeur Elisabeth. "And hurry now to your music lesson. You are late."

Here is an odd thing: I couldn't read music. The notes on a page meant nothing to me. I knew that many people could look at a piece of sheet music and understand exactly how the song should sound, but I couldn't. What I could do was sing perfectly on key once I heard a song. I never forgot music I had learned.

When Madame Marcelle became my tutor, she discovered that I couldn't sight-read. She tried to teach me for a while but soon gave up. "You learn things only in your own way," she said, not disapprovingly. Madame Marcelle was very tall and rather stiff, with gray hair she wore pulled back in a coil. I wasn't sure why everyone called her *madame,* since she wasn't married. I would never have dared to ask. "We'll teach you your own way, then." Madame Marcelle and I got on very well together.

I walked into the music room numb with grief for Madame Montagne and Yvette. My hands were cold. My stomach ached. Madame Marcelle hardly looked at me. "Here is a new song for you," she said. "Bach. J. S. Bach." She stuck the music on a stand in front of me—

she always insisted on putting the music in front of me, as though by osmosis it would somehow begin to make sense—and she sang:

"Magnificat anima mea Dominum . . ."

My soul proclaims the glory of God.

"Magnificat anima mea Dominum . . ." Madame Marcelle's thin voice stretched and soared. Her voice wasn't strong enough for performing, but she could sing. The first part of the piece was a chorus, written for many voices at once.

"Magnificat anima mea . . ."

I knew where it came from, of course. The gospel of Luke, the words Mary's cousin Elizabeth used to greet her when they were both pregnant, Elizabeth with John the Baptist, Mary with Jesus. I thought of Madame Montagne and her little dead baby, and my head swam.

"Magnificat—Suzanne!" Madame Marcelle rapped the music with her pencil. *"Faites attention!* Pay attention! Here is the alto solo. I want you to listen, and then we will get to your part, the soprano." She put her pencil down on the stand and sang again. *"Et exaltavit spiritus meus in Deo salutari meo."*

My spirit rejoices in God my savior.

"Suzanne!"

I grabbed the edge of the music stand to steady myself. I paid attention. We reached my part, and I followed Madame Marcelle's lead. *"Quia respexit humilitatem ancillae suae."* For he has looked upon his lowly one in her distress. *"Ecce enim ex hoc beatam me dicent omnes generationes."* For behold, generations to come will call me blessed.

I sang. The music wrapped around me like a blanket, soft and comforting. I felt safer, singing. I could lose myself in the sound.

There had to be a God, I thought. A vibrant, joyous God in heaven, to make up for the awfulness of what people sometimes did on earth. There had to be a heaven, so that Madame Montagne had a place to go.

CHAPTER THREE

*Y*vette didn't come to school on Friday either. The sisters would not let me telephone her. After school Maman came to pick me up, something she had not done since my first week there. She cradled my face with her hands and looked at me anxiously. "I'm fine," I said. "I'll be fine. Can we go see Yvette?"

At Yvette's house her mother, Madame Gireau, hugged me hard. "My dear, my dear," she murmured, swaying back and forth, "that this should happen to either of you." She pushed me away to arm's length and looked at me. "But you are strong, Suzanne. Stronger than Yvette. Go see if you can get her to talk to you."

Yvette was in the bedroom she shared with her younger sister. She sat in an armchair by the window with her back to the outdoors. She was fully dressed, even down to her shoes, and her hair was combed; she wore a loose gray sweater over her shoulders. She looked neat and clean, and the cut on her cheek was healing. *"Bonjour,"* I said softly.

She said nothing.

"I missed you at school," I said. "I missed you so much. I was worried when you didn't come back." I sat on the edge of the bed, directly in front of her.

She said nothing.

"Are you hurt badly?" I asked. "My arms hurt all the time." Nothing. No words from my best friend. "I pretend they don't hurt," I said. "Odette, Martine—all the girls want to know what happened, and I don't feel like telling them, so I say nothing, and when they ask if my arms hurt, I say, 'No, of course not, why should they?' and they pretty much leave me alone. But I missed you. We can go back together on Monday. I'll come pick you up."

She said nothing. Her face didn't change. She looked at me, and I think she saw me, but she seemed not to understand what I was saying. She seemed not to care.

"They found Simon," I said after a pause. "He was hurt, he was in the square. His head is injured, but Dr. Leclerc says he will live.

"Yvette?" I went on. "Maman says the baby will go to heaven."

Yvette did not move. "Because it had never truly

been born," I explained. "Maman says you don't have to be baptized to go to heaven, if you die before you are truly born. Madame Montagne's baptism counts for the baby too."

Even at this Yvette's face did not change. I talked more, about school and homework and the weather outside—about everything I could think of except the Germans—but I might as well have been talking to a deaf-mute, a polite deaf-mute who did not know me, for all the recognition Yvette showed. After a time I gave her a soft hug—she did not resist—and went away.

At the door Madame Gireau laid her hand on my arm. "Come again," she said. "Come often."

"I will," I said. "I told her I'd come Monday morning and walk with her back to school."

That evening my brothers came home for the weekend too. They were upset that I'd been hurt. "Why did you go near the beach?" Pierre asked. "Don't you have any sense?"

"Quiet," rumbled Papa. "It wasn't her fault."

"But everyone knew about the evacuations," said Etienne.

"I didn't," I said. "What evacuations?"

"Dunkirk," said Papa. "It's over now." He explained what had taken place. I had known that the Germans had crossed the border into France. I hadn't known, until Papa told me, that the German army had advanced with unheard-of speed and slashed a line from one end of France to the other.

The British soldiers, and many of the French, some four hundred thousand men in all, were trapped against the ocean on a very small piece of land at a port city called Dunkirk, about forty kilometers from Cherbourg. Miraculously, nearly all of them were rescued, evacuated across the English Channel to Great Britain, by hundreds and hundreds of boats—fishing vessels, barges, yachts, anything that could float.

"That's why the harbor looked so empty," I said.

"Yes," said Papa. "All our fishermen were helping. It's a victory, after a fashion. At least it's not an overwhelming defeat."

"But what did that have to do with Cherbourg?" I asked. "Why did they bomb the square?"

"I don't know," Papa said. He shook his head. "I don't know."

"She should have known better," persisted Etienne. "She could have been—"

"Quiet," Papa said. "She knows."

⌒ᴧ

Saturday Maman and I went to the market, which was near the Place Napoléon. I carried one big market basket, and Maman carried the other. I had always loved going to the market with my mother, especially on a bright spring day. The wind whipped little white-caps on the surface of the sea, and the sun glinted on the cobblestones.

The Place Napoléon was pockmarked with craters from the bombs. As we approached, my head turned as if by its own accord to the bench where Yvette and I had sat, to the spot where Madame Montagne had died. The bench was still there. An old man sat on it, enjoying a cigarette, his legs crossed and his arms flung back. The stones in front of it had been scrubbed clean; not a trace of that dark pool of blood remained.

I thought I would vomit. My hands began to shake.

"Oh, my love," Maman said softly. "We shouldn't have come this way."

"No. It's nothing. I'm fine."

I walked across the square. I went to the market. I helped Maman pick out fish for dinner and a leg of lamb for Sunday, and I watched the butter dealer carve half a kilo of butter off his great yellow mound. He held it out to me wrapped in a leaf of lettuce, and I put it in my basket. Maman bought some of the first tender peas of the year. I felt numb. Grief sank into my belly like a stone.

The next day was Sunday. As usual, my widowed aunt Suzanne and her six children came to dinner after Mass. I loved my cousins, but they were all younger than me; there was not one of an age to be my friend. Whenever they came to our house Papa always said, "Here comes your aunt Suzanne and her battalion," so that was how I thought of them.

Some days the battalion overwhelmed me. On this Sunday I thought they certainly would. But when my first small cousin cried, "Suzanne!" and launched herself into my lap, I was surprised at how tightly I hugged her in return. I carried her around part of the afternoon and put her down only to pick up another. My cousins hung on my legs and climbed over me, and I put my face into their hair and breathed deeply, and began to feel better.

"Sing to us," little Isabelle said. "Sing, sing."

I began an Ave. Isabelle shook her head. "Sing something interesting."

The children's song that came to mind was the cabbage song Yvette had sung on the way to the beach. I thought of Yvette laughing. I couldn't sing. Aunt Suzanne must have seen my face, because she came and took Isabelle away. "Come, come, the lamb is ready," she said. "The lamb and the flageolets. Sit down."

CHAPTER FOUR

$\mathcal{O}$n Monday we were beginning our end-of-the-year exams when we heard that the Germans had bombed Paris. After dinner the sisters took us to the chapel and led us in saying a rosary. *Je vous salue, Marie, pleine de grâce* . . . Hail Mary, full of grace . . . I thought of my two uncles who lived in Paris and added a special prayer for their safety. Then I thought of Yvette. I closed my eyes and dedicated a decade of my rosary to her.

Yvette wasn't taking her exams. Yvette had not come back to school.

I had gone to her house especially early that morning in case she wasn't quite ready. When I knocked, her mother took a long time to come to the door. "Oh, it's you, Suzanne," she said when she saw me. She sounded tired. Her hair was not yet combed. "Yvette had a difficult night," she said. She smiled wistfully and stepped aside so I could enter. "Do you have nightmares too?"

I had nightmares, but I didn't wish to trouble Madame Gireau with them. "May I speak to Yvette?"

"She's sleeping, little one. I don't want to wake her."

"But school—"

"Suzanne, dear child." Madame Gireau put her hand on my shoulder. "She cannot go to school right now."

⌒

So now Paris had been bombed. After our rosary the sisters led us to a quiet supper and then to study time. Only when we were back in our rooms preparing for bed could we speak freely at last. "Think of the cathedral, beautiful Notre Dame," said Odette. "It has stood for so many hundreds of years. I pray it wasn't hit."

"Of course it wasn't hit," Martine said. "Don't be a ninny. They would have told us if Notre Dame was hit." Four of us shared one room—Odette, Martine, Colette, and me.

"Oh, but think of all the beautiful old buildings," Odette moaned. "The museums—the Louvre. It would be such a tragedy. Think of the history."

I had often wished Yvette were one of my roommates. I wished it more now, listening to Odette yammer on. I wondered if Yvette had felt better after she had woken up that day.

"It should be against the law," Odette declared. "They shouldn't be allowed to bomb Paris."

I said bitterly, "But to bomb Cherbourg, now, that's all right."

The others went silent. Odette plumped her pillow. Martine bit her lip. After a pause Colette spoke. "What was it like last week? You haven't said anything. What happened?"

"Nothing," I said. I climbed into my cot. "It was like nothing." I turned my face to the wall.

⌒〜ᴧ

At the end of that week school was over for the year. Ordinarily I loved summer. I loved the warm sun and the breezes, I loved shopping with Maman and spending days on Aunt Suzanne's farm. But now we lived under a cloud of worry. The German army approached Paris. New grass was sprouting on Madame Montagne's grave. Yvette still didn't speak. I walked home slowly, my books held to my chest.

Maman and I were drinking tea in the kitchen when Papa came home. His face looked gray and tired. "Is there news?" Maman asked.

He shook his head. "I think waiting is the hardest part," he said.

Maman said, "I hope so."

~~~

It turned out that even Hitler was reluctant to destroy Paris's beauty. The Germans bombed the city only once, and none of the famous buildings was harmed.

A week later, on the fourteenth of June, with the German army growing ever nearer, the French government declared Paris an open city. This meant that France would not defend it in exchange for the Germans' not destroying it. We gave Paris to the Nazis. I believe it pleased Hitler to see the German flag fly over the Eiffel Tower. One of the last photos in the Cherbourg newspaper before the Germans took it over showed just that: Hitler, the Eiffel Tower, the German flag. Millions of people—more than three-quarters of the population—fled Paris. My two uncles stayed.

"A sad day for *la belle* France," Papa said, slapping that newspaper down on the dinner table. Pierre and I sat silent on our side of the table. Etienne played with his fork on the tablecloth.

"I didn't think it could happen to France," Etienne said. "If I were a soldier . . ." His voice trailed off.

None of us responded. Etienne would never be a

soldier, even though Papa had been in the cavalry in Paris, even though Papa's commanding officer, the great General Charles de Gaulle, was Etienne's own godfather. Four years ago Etienne had slipped running down Aunt Suzanne's spiral staircase. He had fallen all the way to the bottom and broken his back. On good days he walked with crutches. Other times he used a wheelchair. Etienne was brave and intelligent and never complained, even though he still had a great deal of pain. If I was tough, I got it from him.

"I'll be a soldier," Pierre declared. "I'll fight Hitler, that dirty pig!"

"You will be a schoolboy," Papa replied. "You will do just as you should, and you will not be hurt."

"I want to be a soldier," Pierre said.

"A soldier listens to orders," said Papa. He pointed at Pierre with his cigarette. "A soldier does as he is told."

⌣‿ᴧ

Every battleship in Cherbourg's harbor had either sailed for England or been sunk on purpose to prevent it from falling into enemy hands. The Germans were very close.

On Sunday Marshal Pétain became premier of France. We heard it on the radio. Papa swore. "Don't you like General Pétain?" I asked. He had been a hero in the Great War.

"He is an old man," Papa said. "He had courage once but he does not have it now." Papa leaned back in his chair. "Pétain is afraid of the Germans," he continued. "For years General de Gaulle has said we should prepare for war. For years de Gaulle urged us to take the German threat seriously. Did we listen? No. Did we prepare? No. And now we are overrun."

"Where is General de Gaulle now?" asked Etienne.

Papa looked grim. "I don't know."

⌣⌐

The German army, led by General Rommel, approached Cherbourg. What was left of the French army fought hard to defend us. As the battle drew nearer, the sounds of bombs and shooting grew louder from the hills behind the city. To me they were echoes of the day at the Place Napoléon. I worried about Papa, who was at his job in the railroad station. I worried about Pierre, who had run off somewhere. I worried about myself, about all of us. A bomb could strike anywhere.

"Be still," Maman said. "You wiggle too much." She was pinning pieces of a dress around me to see how they would fit. Maman was a wonderful seamstress. She made most of my clothes.

"I must visit Yvette," I said. I went to see her nearly every day. A day earlier I had thought she'd almost spoken.

Etienne was in the parlor, listening to the radio. From far away gunfire sounded like firecrackers. My hands shook, the tiniest bit.

"Today you stay here," Maman replied.

"But Yvette—"

"You stay here," Maman said. "Do you understand?" Maman almost never spoke so sharply.

"Yes, Maman."

Etienne came into the room on his crutches. "Listen," he said. He nodded at the window. "Open it, Suzanne."

I opened it and we listened. It was a steady hum of engines, a rumble of machinery. "Tanks," said Etienne. "I think we have surrendered."

⌒〜

When Papa came home he said it was true. Cherbourg was in German hands. The city officials had surrendered. The railroad had been given to the Germans.

"Surely you don't work for the Nazis, Papa?" Pierre asked.

"I do," Papa said. "The Germans need a dispatcher. They may have control of the railroad, but they don't know how to run it."

Pierre scowled. I could read his thoughts on his face.

So could Papa, for he put his hands on the table and said, very slowly, "I had two choices, my son. The German commander explained them carefully to me. I could continue to work as I have always done, receive my pay, as I have always done, and provide for my family, as I have always done. Or I could be shot and killed." Papa spread his hands. "Which would you have had me choose?"

I looked at Maman and saw that her lips were trembling. I felt strangely calm. I could feel a small square piece of shrapnel embedded in my arm. It reminded me, whenever I managed to forget, how bad war could be.

"You made the right choice, Papa," Etienne said.

"Of course I did," Papa roared. "Haven't I told you? Obey the rules and no one gets hurt."

"But Papa—" I began. Madame Montagne, Yvette, and I had not broken the rules.

"You are a smart girl," Papa said. "Use your head. Obeying them gives us our best chance. Cherbourg belongs to the Germans now."

⌒◟

They came for our house the next day.

CHAPTER FIVE

It was a Wednesday. Papa had come home for his noontime dinner, and we were all sitting down for the meal. The Germans did not knock. They tried to open the front door, and when the latch stuck, as it sometimes did, they slammed something hard down upon it and broke it. I heard a crash, and then another, and the slam of the door against the hallway wall, and the faint sounds of the clock chimes echoing in response. Pierre and I flew up from our chairs. Etienne grabbed for his crutches, but Maman and Papa did not move. They sat frozen, their faces carefully blank.

Pierre ran into the hall. I followed. He stopped so suddenly that I bumped against his back. Two German soldiers stood in our hallway, their guns pointed straight at Pierre's stomach. One of them made a motion with the barrel of the gun, and Pierre, who was taller than the soldier, put his hands above his head.

A third German, dressed as an officer, stood beside the first two. He looked into our parlor, with its beautiful mural, its fine furniture, and Maman's piano. He looked into the dining room, where we had been eating our meal. He looked at the carpet and the wallpaper, and he smiled to himself. "Get out!" he roared in heavily accented French. "Hurry! Gather your things. You can take what you can carry."

Maman and Papa were in the hallway by now. For a moment none of us moved. "Thirty minutes!" said the German officer. He glanced at the big clock in the hall. "Go!"

Without a word to each other we sprang into action. Papa went to his desk in the parlor and began to dump papers into his briefcase. Maman ran up the stairs, the boys and I at her heels. I ran into my room. I didn't know what to take. How long would we be gone? Where would we be going?

Every moment I agonized was another moment gone. I took my schoolbag off the floor and crammed some of my books into it. My hairbrush, my best hat. I pulled clothes out of my dresser and stuffed my suitcase full.

Maman appeared in the doorway. "Take your winter coat," she said. "We don't know how hard it will be to get you another." She watched me for a moment. "Don't panic," she said. "It'll be all right."

I had no room for the coat in my suitcase. I put the coat on my bed, on top of the pretty spread Maman had made for me. Suddenly I knew the Germans could not have that too. I laid more clothing on top of my coat and gathered the edges of the spread together to make a bundle. It was awkward, but I could carry it.

Papa came bounding up the stairs, a wooden box under one arm and a green and white china demitasse cup in his hand. The box contained our silver set, which had been my grandmother's. The cup was part of a set Papa had given to Maman that year. Maman smiled at him. "I have a box," she said. "I think we will take the whole set." She carried the cup downstairs and began to pack the demitasse cups and saucers in a box padded with kitchen towels. I followed her.

"Do we need our pots and pans?" I asked.

Maman shrugged. Her self-control amazed me. "I suppose so," she said. "We must have necessities, and we should take whatever is valuable that the Germans might steal. I think the everyday things—the personal things—we can come back for."

Papa and Pierre were stacking parcels on the curb. I went back to my room and took my gold-rimmed First Communion cup off my shelf. I wouldn't want the Germans to sell it. I nestled it carefully inside my suitcase.

The other things I treasured—my movie star photos, my ribbons and music and books, my photograph of the singer Tino Rossi—would be worthless to the Germans. I could come back for them. But I took some more clothing and carried it downstairs, and I took our toothbrushes and Papa's razor from the bath. I helped Maman choose the essentials from the kitchen. Papa carried Maman's sewing machine outside.

"Time!" shouted the German in the hallway.

We straggled into the hallway, all carrying one last thing. Etienne had a satchel on his back. "You have my wheelchair?" he asked Pierre. Pierre nodded.

"Good," the German said when we were assembled. "Now I need your house keys."

I didn't understand why they needed keys when they had smashed the lock. Papa put his suitcase down, searched in his pocket, and removed the keys from his chain. I looked into the dining room. Our dinner sat on our plates, the cider in Papa's and Maman's glasses hardly touched. I wondered if the Germans would eat our food after we had gone.

"My bicycle," Pierre said suddenly. I gulped. We both had fine bicycles. I loved mine. They were in the garden shed.

The officer laughed. "I don't think you can carry a bicycle," he said. Something in his tone frightened me. Pierre dropped his eyes.

I looked toward the garden anyway. There was my new dress, the one Maman had made me, hanging on the line. "Sir," I said to the officer, "my dress—" He frowned. I didn't think he understood me. "Outside," I said, pointing.

He strode to the back door, opened it, and looked out. Then he laughed, a hard, vicious laugh. "Yes, of course, *mademoiselle*," he said with an extravagant sweep of his arm. "We wouldn't wish you to be without *those*."

When I went out to the garden I understood his laughter. On the line beside my dress hung a row of my white underwear.

I gathered it all up and took the clothespins too.

Maman and Papa and Pierre were already on the front walk, but Etienne had waited for me. I carried the wet laundry through our house, looking neither right nor left. One of the soldiers snickered as I went by.

"Chin up," Etienne murmured in French.

As he spoke, one of the soldiers stuck his foot between Etienne's leg and the tip of his crutch. Etienne fell hard. He gasped in pain.

I knelt beside him and took hold of his arm. He pulled away. "I'll do it," he said. "Nobody helps me. I'll do it myself."

One of the soldiers said something mocking in German. It was easy to guess what he meant even though I couldn't understand the words. *Cripple.* I whirled around, wanting to slap him.

"Suzanne," Etienne said softly, "don't. It will make things worse." He was on his knees now, struggling with his crutches. Gradually he pulled himself to his feet. My knees trembled as I followed him out the door. He was better than they were; he was brave and good. But they had our house.

All up and down the street we saw German soldiers. All up and down the street our neighbors were being turned out of their homes too. A few houses away Dr. Leclerc stood on the sidewalk, waving his hands in the air as he talked to a German officer. His son played in the grass near his feet. Dr. Leclerc raised his eyebrows briefly at my father.

"Well," said Maman slowly, "now I'll believe anything."

"Papa," said Etienne, "where do we go?"

CHAPTER SIX

*T*he Germans took over the houses on only two streets in Cherbourg: Rue Lohen, which was ours, and Rue Loubet, which ran parallel to it. They also took over the hotel and the château, and some city buildings downtown, for their headquarters and officers' barracks. Our street housed regular troops.

"*Sales Boches,*" Maman sniffed. "Dirty Germans. *Sales cochons,* those dirty pigs. In my nice clean house."

Maman didn't seem afraid of the Nazis. She seemed ready to fight them.

Monsieur and Madame Herbert, friends who lived a few blocks away, took us in. They fed us and said we could sleep in their basement until we found a place of our own. "We'll find somewhere else as soon as we can," Papa said, shaking his head.

Monsieur Herbert lit a cigarette and gave it to him.

"Yes, of course," he said. "But tonight you can stay here."

"Tonight, yes, thank you," Papa said. He looked at his watch. "And I'm late getting back for work. I must go." He forced a smile. "Otherwise the German dogs might fire me."

Meanwhile Madame Herbert rearranged the things stored in her basement to make room for our belongings. She had a small bed for my parents to sleep on, and she brought down blankets and pillows and helped my brothers and me make up beds on the floor.

It was generous of the Herberts, I know. But their basement was damp and musty. The Germans ordered everyone to hang blackout curtains over their windows so that Allied fighters could not see Cherbourg from the night sky. When Madame Herbert hung one over the tiny basement window, it felt as though we were living in a cave.

"I wish they'd let us have their parlor," Pierre grumbled.

"They would let us," Papa said. "I wouldn't take it. We must impose on them as little as possible. Who knows how long we'll have to stay here?"

Pierre shrugged behind Papa's back, as if to say, *How long could it take?* I shrugged back. I didn't know.

I wished I had brought my baby album. The next

morning I decided to see if I could get it from our house. Without saying anything to Maman, I walked the few blocks back to our street. It was barricaded, and the barricade was guarded by Nazi soldiers.

"Please," I said quietly, "I would like to fetch some things from my old house. Some personal things. I'll only take a moment."

The guards, two young men with large guns, looked at each other and said something in German. One laughed. Then the other waved his gun down the street and said something to me in German that I didn't understand.

I could feel my heart beating harder. I could feel my cheeks begin to turn red.

"Pardon me," I said. "May I please go to my old house?"

Again a German response. I didn't think they understood French. "Right there," I said, pointing. "That is my house, right there."

The soldiers looked, smiled, and pointed. "All right, then?" I said. "Is it all right?" I started to step through the barricade.

"Nein!" the first soldier said. He pushed me backward so hard that I fell to the ground. At least he used his hand to push me, not his gun. *"Nein!"* He said more, an angry torrent of words, all in German. I

didn't understand the words, but I understood their meaning. I couldn't go home.

"Oh, Suzanne," Maman cried when I told her about it later. "How could you put yourself in danger for a few photographs? You mustn't think about the things we left behind. They will be there when we return."

⌒ᴧ

I don't know why Papa thought it would be so hard to find another place to live, but he was right; it was. We stayed with the Herberts for over three weeks. Meanwhile France signed a peace treaty with Nazi Germany. It divided our country into two parts: occupied France, where we lived, which was under the control of the German army, and Vichy France, the southern part, which had its own puppet French government under Hitler's control. I was glad not to live in Vichy France, even if life was easier there. Papa called the Vichy government traitors, and I thought they were too.

Now there were many restricted areas in Cherbourg where only the Germans could go. Now we all had to turn in our radios. Etienne heard that some people were digging holes to hide their radios in their gardens, but since our radio was in our old house we didn't have that choice. We were allowed to keep our cameras only as long as we didn't use them—if German soldiers saw someone taking a photograph, they took that person's camera and kept it. We were not allowed to send mail outside France. The newspapers printed nothing but German propaganda. In the space of two weeks it became very difficult to know how the war was going. It became impossible to learn the truth.

One Saturday morning Maman and I walked down to the marketplace, only to find it empty. A scattering of soldiers chased would-be shoppers away. "Go home, *madame*," one of them called to Maman. "The market is closed. There is no more Saturday market. Go home."

"Why would they take away the market?" I asked.

Maman looked weary. "There could be harm in a market," she said. "So many French people all together in one place—there could be harm in a market, Suzanne."

I did not understand.

It was hot. The Herberts were tired of us, and we were tired of them. One day Madame Herbert asked Maman if I could please not practice singing that day. Madame Herbert had a headache, and my scales were so loud.

It was all I could do not to slam the door of Madame Herbert's house. She got to keep her house. She could let me sing. I went to Madame Marcelle's apartment. "May I sing here?" I asked.

Madame Marcelle pushed back a lace curtain to open the window wider. "Of course, my dear," she said. "It is always a pleasure to hear you sing. I'm glad you thought to come." She sat down on her sofa and smiled. "Sing all you like," she said. "Sing anytime."

⌒

To Yvette I sang the cabbage song. I thought it might jolt her out of her indifference. It didn't. I might as well have been singing in Swahili.

Of all the sadness the war had brought, Yvette was the worst for me. I still went to see her often, but I dreaded it more and more. Yvette's poor mother looked tired and defeated. "Come again," she always said, and I always promised, "I will."

⌒

Finally Papa found us a place to live. "It's a good little apartment," he said. He held up his hands. "Four rooms, and a nice little closet where Suzanne can sleep."

A closet! I was horrified. But poor Maman and Papa seemed so weary, and we were all so tired of the Herberts' basement, that I held my tongue. The Herberts helped us carry our belongings through town. Papa stopped on the edge of the cemetery.

Pierre joked, "I'd rather sleep among the living, thanks." Maman smacked his arm.

"There," said Papa, nodding toward a rickety house overlooking the graveyard. "The second floor."

The apartment had a kitchen, a living room, a tiny bath, and two bedrooms. My closet was an alcove off the kitchen, meant to be a pantry. It was barely big enough for a cot. The walls were yellowed, and every inch of the floor was filthy; a smell of old grease hung in the air. I lifted the stained curtain from the kitchen window and saw fresh graves dug in the cemetery. I closed my eyes and remembered the clean prettiness of Maman's parlor, of my own room. Then I opened my eyes. This was the best Papa could do. I dropped the curtain and turned around.

"We'll make it better," Maman said cheerfully.

"The bed will look nice with my spread on it," I replied. "It'll cheer up the whole room."

"It'll *be* the whole room," muttered Pierre.

"We can make curtains," Maman said.

"Pah!" said Papa. "It isn't a good place." He sat down on the sagging couch in the main room. The apartment was furnished, sort of. "It's the best we can do, so we'll make it do, that's all. But I have good news too."

He waited until we were all listening. "General de Gaulle is safe in England," he said. "He is organizing a government there. The Free French."

"How do you know?" Pierre asked.

"Pah! I know. Don't ask questions," Papa said.

"How can he run France from England?" asked Etienne. "He doesn't have any power."

"Power, no, but he has authority," Papa said. "The Allies will listen to him. They will let him make decisions that might help us later on." Papa shook his head. "De Gaulle is a good man, the best we have. It's a blessing he is among the Allies."

⁓

Supper that night was an old fish our new landlord had not wanted, and rutabagas Etienne found when he went to the shops late in the day. We did not have enough plates, so Maman put my food into a bowl. "Only for tonight," she murmured. "Tomorrow we will find another." Even with her kindness it was such a contrast to our usual meals that I pushed the bowl away.

"Eat," Papa said.

"I can't eat," I said.

"Suzanne, for shame," murmured Maman.

"They have taken everything," I burst out. "They took our house, they took our food, they took our bicycles—"

Papa put up his hand. I ignored him. "Madame Montagne's *life*—"

Papa's hand came down on mine, softly, not hard. "They have not taken anything that matters," he said.

"Madame Montagne," I whispered furiously.

"No," said Papa, "our lives belong to the Lord. The Nazis have not taken our work, Suzanne. They have not taken your voice. They have not taken our courage or our faith. We haven't lost anything of value."

Pierre and Etienne stared at their plates. I pulled my bowl closer and picked up my fork.

"We will continue," said Papa. "We will be strong. Eat your supper, Suzanne."

I ate.

CHAPTER SEVEN

*M*aman and I cleaned the cemetery apartment. She tried to make it look cheerful, but the ugly, ramshackle furniture and our few possessions kept me longing for home. Every day I remembered something else left behind: my scooter, my dressing gown, my favorite dolls, outgrown but still beloved. I went to our street once more. It remained barricaded. I didn't go back after that.

On Sunday Aunt Suzanne and the battalion came as always. Aunt Suzanne must have said something to my young cousins to silence them, because not one of them so much as mentioned the fact that we were living somewhere different. They looked around with wide eyes, but they didn't say a word. Pierre took them outside to play soccer in the graveyard.

"So," said Aunt Suzanne, sitting down at the table, "it will do."

I was pleased she had not said something untrue, like *It's not so bad*.

"I couldn't get lamb," Maman informed her. The rationing was becoming more strict. "Dinner is only a poor piece of beef."

"So, then," said Aunt Suzanne again, "it will do." She turned to me. "Will you sing for us, little Suzanne?"

"Of course." I closed my eyes and imagined myself not in the apartment but in Madame Marcelle's clean, bright home, where there was always room for me to sing. I sang the Magnificat she had taught me.

"Beautiful," Aunt Suzanne said when I had finished.

In many ways our apartment was not as nice even as the Herberts' basement, but at least it was somewhere I could sing. I smiled at Aunt Suzanne. I said, "It will do."

⌒

I often saw German soldiers march by. Civilians scuttled out of their way. A few days after we moved to the cemetery I saw a French soldier for the first time since the Germans took over. His name was Guillaume, he was my roommate Odette's older brother, and he was dressed in civilian clothes. I knew he had been a lieutenant. I started to call out his name, but he shot me a look of such alarm and walked past so brusquely that I stopped short and stared at him.

Then I realized what I had almost done. If the Germans knew he had been a soldier, they would capture him. They would take him to a war camp, who knew where.

At night when I told my family about Guillaume, Papa in particular looked grave. "You must always be on guard," he said. His look swept the table. "All of you, all of the time."

"There was a German soldier behind me in the bakery today," Pierre said. "He came in so quietly that I didn't know he was there until I turned around."

"Yes," said Papa. "So it's lucky you weren't making jokes about the Germans. You must be careful what you say, whether or not you can see soldiers. You never know what people might do." He took a bite of supper. "There are rumors of spies," he said. "Men and women both, dressed in civilian clothes, who speak perfect French. You would never know them for Nazis, not at all."

"Be careful," Maman said quietly. "Be careful always."

⌒ⵠ

"Why so quiet today?" Madame Marcelle asked one summer afternoon. I had gone for a singing lesson, but we had finished and were having a cup of tea. Madame Marcelle was telling me the story of the opera

Rigoletto. She sang bits of it. The sea breeze fluttered through her lace curtains.

"Pardon, *madame?*" I looked up. I had been listening closely to the *Rigoletto* story. I didn't know what she meant.

"You were much livelier six months ago," she said. "Are you still enjoying your singing?"

"More than anything," I said. I studied the pattern on the teacup in my hand. I loved Madame Marcelle's apartment. Nothing in it ever changed. Sitting in it, you would never know there was a war.

"You don't mind the work? Singing is harder the more serious you become."

"I never mind work," I said. "I like hard things. If I am quiet, it's because of everything that isn't singing."

Madame Marcelle waited, watching me.

"I went to Yvette's house this morning," I said. "She still doesn't speak to me, or to anyone, not even her mother. So today I tried to make her angry at me. I tried to make her lose her temper and shout at me." I looked up at my teacher. "She used to do that, you know. Not very often, but once I told her that her new hat looked like a bag of pudding, and she told me I was the daughter of a goat and my singing sounded like sheep who were trying to yodel."

Madame smiled. I didn't. I played with the fringe on the edge of her sofa cushion. "I told her she was a coward," I said. "I told her she was letting the Nazis win, letting them kill her just as they killed Madame Montagne. I told her she was weak and selfish and afraid."

"And then?" asked Madame Marcelle.

"Nothing. She looked at me as though I were there to clean the carpet. Only she isn't a coward. I know Yvette; I know she must be doing the best she can. I am the coward, to say such things to someone who is hurting as much as she is."

"You're not a coward," Madame Marcelle said. "You are fearless when you sing."

I nearly laughed. "See? That must be why I sing."

⌒ᴧ

We were forbidden, of course, to fly the French flag—the tricolor, blue, white, and red—or to sing the national anthem or show any sign of patriotism toward France. We didn't disobey. As Papa said, we weren't that stupid. But one day Etienne came to lunch with three pencils lined up in his shirt pocket, a blue pencil, a white one, and a red one. Blue, white, red.

"What is that?" thundered Papa.

"What?" asked Etienne, startled. I think he had forgotten the pencils.

"That in your pocket—that, you know."

Etienne looked down. "Oh, that." He smiled and ran his finger across the tops of the pencils. "I needed some new pencils, Papa, that's all. I thought these looked like good ones. Don't you agree?"

Papa stared at Etienne's bland expression for a long moment before laughing. When Papa laughed, the rest of us did too. "And if the Germans ask you, that's just what you say," he told Etienne. " 'I needed some pencils,' *hein?* You hadn't noticed anything about their colors."

"Of course not, Papa," said Etienne. "What would there be to notice? They're only pencils."

<hr/>

All around, things were not what they seemed. German spies spoke perfect French; pencils held a secret message. Meanwhile I did nothing useful. I sang, I helped Maman. I still visited Yvette, but not so often. Seeing her hurt my heart.

"I would like to be a help to someone," I told Maman.

"Good," she said. "Scrub those rutabagas for me, and then you can hem the skirt of that dress I'm making."

I preferred to do something more adventurous. "If I eat another rutabaga," I declared, "I will die."

"I'm sorry your life is to be cut so short," Maman replied. "I hope you will be able to finish the skirt before dinner so that you'll have something nice to wear when you are lying in your casket."

"Maman!"

"Oh, Suzanne," Maman said, laughing. "We can't take everything seriously, can we? Even now."

Instead of making me scrub the rutabagas, Maman told me to go down to the docks and get some fish for dinner. Beef, sugar, butter, flour, and many other foods had become scarce, but in Cherbourg we could always get fresh fish. The Nazis still allowed French fishermen to earn their living as long as they stuck to coastal waters.

"I'll go too," Pierre declared. I rolled my eyes, but he came anyway.

It was a warm, slightly overcast day. We walked quickly through the streets. "Oh, look," said Pierre. "There's Monsieur Vardin." He was a prominent local man, quite well-off and educated. We sometimes saw him at church, and I knew Papa had great respect for him.

"What's that on his arm?" I asked. Monsieur Vardin wore a white armband, like the black ones people wore for mourning, only much more noticeable, over his brown suit. I read it. "RAF?"

"You've got to be kidding," said Pierre.

Clearly printed on the armband were the letters

RAF. The only RAF I knew was the Royal Air Force, the British fighter pilots, our allies. Surely Monsieur Vardin would not wear such a thing in public?

"*Bonjour,* children," he said cheerily to us as we passed him.

"*Bonjour, monsieur,*" we replied. I couldn't bring myself to ask him what his armband meant. Neither, I supposed, could Pierre, for he said nothing.

We had barely gone three steps farther when we heard a harsh shout. "You there! Old man!"

We whirled around. Pierre put a steadying hand on my arm. Two German soldiers stood in front of Monsieur Vardin. "What is this?" one shouted, jabbing the armband. "RAF? What is this?"

"Oh, that." Monsieur Vardin lifted his hands and shrugged expressively. He didn't seem at all afraid. "Pardon, *messieurs.* This rationing, it's so hard on an old man. The armband stands for *rien à fumer,* 'nothing to smoke,' because I am out of cigarettes. I'm hoping that if I advertise my unfortunate predicament, someone who still has cigarettes might take pity on me."

He said this so seriously that the soldiers didn't know what to think. I bit my lip and struggled not to laugh.

"Hmpf." One of the soldiers dug into his jacket pocket. He tossed a pack of cigarettes to Monsieur

Vardin. "Here you go, then. But get rid of the armband."

~~~∿~~~

Pierre had a paper route and so he was out on the streets quite often. One night he came home shaking with laughter. He told us the story at dinner. "You know Monsieur Vardin and his RAF armband?" he said. "Well, I saw him wearing it again today. And the Nazis stopped him again, and they said, 'We told you to get rid of that armband,' and he said, 'Oh, pardon, *messieurs,* it's not the same armband. This one stands for *remerciement au Führer pour les cigarettes,'* "—thanks to Hitler for the cigarettes.

"So what did they do?" I asked.

"Gave him more cigarettes. But I think he'll have to leave the armband off now."

~~~∿~~~

Such things were funny, but many other things weren't. The cigarette ration was hard on Papa, who had always smoked. Wine was rationed. My parents usually drank cider during the week, but soon they drank it even on Sundays. There was no candy. "I would do anything for a bite of chocolate," I told my school roommate Martine. She had come to spend the day with us late in August, just before school began.

"Anything?" she asked.

"Anything," I said.

"Would you kiss a German soldier?"

"*Martine!* Never! Of course not!"

"Would you speak to one?"

"Not if I could help it," I said.

"Not even for a whole bar of chocolate? If you just had to say, 'Excuse me, I'd like some of that chocolate,' would you?" she asked.

I thought of the Germans living in my house, sleeping on my bed under the photo of Tino Rossi on the wall. I thought of Yvette's blank face, Yvette's mother's sadness. "No," I said. "I would not."

Martine shook her head. "Me either," she said.

"Well," I said fiercely, "that's good. Because I'll tell you something, Martine—if you had answered differently, I'm not sure I could still be your friend." Martine smiled at me but looked a little surprised by my tone. I wasn't joking, not at all.

We had been walking through the cemetery by our apartment. It was a good place for private conversations. Martine bent and gently rearranged the flowers that someone had left on a loved one's grave. "When the war is over," she said, "I'm never eating rutabagas again."

I laughed. "Oh, Martine," I said, "I think we'll be friends for a long, long time."

⌒〜

Our daily lives went on. I would have liked to believe that shortages of chocolate and cigarettes and flour were the worst things we had to endure. But I started to notice something frightening: Sometimes people disappeared.

CHAPTER EIGHT

I didn't realize it at first. I hadn't known it could happen. Around the time that school began again, the Nazis passed the first of their laws restricting the activities of French Jews. At the same time they banned books by Jewish authors from the stores.

"They threw the books into the streets," Madame Marcelle told me at my singing lesson. "They burned them. If the author was a Jew." Her voice was tight with anger.

"Are there operas written by Jewish people?" I asked. I didn't know of any. Not Mozart, not Verdi, not Bizet.

"What difference does that make?" Madame Marcelle asked. Now she sounded angry with me.

"None," I said. "I mean, it won't make a difference, will it, if it doesn't affect what I can sing? Or what I learn at school?"

"It makes a difference," she said. "Suzanne, think."

I thought, because she wanted me to. "Like the newspaper," I said. "How it's only propaganda now. The Nazis are trying to control what we can read."

Madame Marcelle shook her head. "It's much worse than that," she said. "Controlling the newspaper makes sense in an occupied land. Novels and works of literature are art in the same way that songs are art. It's wrong to burn them. It's wrong to ban them."

I could see that it might be wrong, but I couldn't see why Madame Marcelle was so upset. She shrugged, sighed, and set me to learning a new Alleluia to sing for Christmas.

I had the same roommates again for the new school year. In the dormitory late at night I asked them what they thought about the new rules.

"It doesn't hurt us, does it?" said Odette.

"How can we know?" I asked. "Madame Marcelle thinks it can."

"Everyone in Cherbourg is Catholic," said Odette. "I've never even seen a Jew."

"No," said Martine. "Maman said she knew of one, but not in Cherbourg."

"I know a Protestant," offered Colette.

"A Jewish family lives near my uncles in Paris," I said.

"What do they look like?" asked Colette.

"Same as us," I said. "You can't tell they're Jewish by

looking at them." So maybe I understood Madame Marcelle after all.

Not far from our apartment there lived a man who operated a taxi service from his home. Automobiles were rare in town, so he was always busy. He and his wife and children all had dark skin; they were one of the few black families in Cherbourg. One Friday when I was walking home from school, I saw his taxi parked in front of his house. This was strange; he usually worked quite late on Fridays. I hoped he wasn't sick.

On Monday morning when I passed his house, the taxi was still parked in the same spot. A few leaves had blown onto the windshield. It didn't look as though the car had been moved.

I didn't think about the taxi driver all week, but on Friday, as I was walking home again, I saw that the taxi was still parked on the curb, more leaves fallen onto the windshield and hood.

I felt a little chill run through me. There was something not right about the taxi. Why hadn't anyone driven it? The taxi was the man's livelihood; surely if he were sick, he would have found someone to drive it for him.

Without really knowing why, I ripped a sheet of paper out of my notebook. I stuck it against the windshield, tucked under one of the wipers. Anyone driving the car would take the paper off first.

On Monday morning the paper was still there. The

car looked dirtier and more forlorn. The little garden in front of the man's house was filling with dead leaves. I walked to school with an anxious lump in my throat.

"Do you know the taxi driver?" I asked Soeur Elisabeth.

She shook her head. "We never take taxis," she said. "Why? What's wrong?"

"I don't know," I said.

Odette and Colette thought it was strange that I should be so worried about a man I'd never spoken to, whose name I didn't even know. Martine didn't say she thought it was strange, but she didn't seem to understand. Yvette would have, I thought. Yvette had cared about everyone before she fell apart.

That night as I tried to go to sleep I spoke in my mind to the old Yvette, the one who always had answers to my questions. *A taxi driver could be useful to the Germans, the way my father is useful. They wouldn't do anything to a useful person, would they?*

No one answered me now. On Friday when I walked home again, I gathered my courage and peeked into the window of the taxi driver's house. I saw a room left in disorder, children's toys scattered about, a baby blanket in a heap on the floor. The blanket chilled me. They could not have meant to leave it behind.

I ran home and told my parents what I had seen. They shook their heads and looked grave.

"Where do you think they went?" I asked. "What do you think happened?"

Papa sighed. "I think they disappeared," he said. "I think it will be better if you don't ask questions."

"Better?" My voice rose in a shriek.

"Better for you," Papa said. "Not better for them. I don't think anything we could do would be either better or worse for them. At this point, Suzanne, we can do nothing to help them. I doubt whether we ever could have."

I felt like crying, but I wouldn't. "I thought Hitler only hated Jews," I said. "I didn't know he hated black people too."

Papa was smoking black-market cigarettes, which stained his fingers yellow. He rolled a pencil between his yellow fingers. "Now you do."

It was months before someone hauled the taxi away. After a few weeks I began to walk back and forth to school by a different route so that I wouldn't have to see it. Meanwhile I sang and sang, Alleluias and Glorias and operatic arias, and in the chapel every morning I prayed and prayed and prayed.

CHAPTER NINE

The winter of 1940 was bleak and cold. My little cousins kept getting sick, one after another. Their illnesses weren't serious, but they kept Aunt Suzanne from visiting us, or us from visiting them. I hadn't realized how much I would miss them.

Now fuel had gotten expensive. Papa could afford to heat our little apartment, but the school was cold all the time. My brothers were cold too in their monastery school. Maman sent us all off with extra blankets and made sure we had warm socks, but she couldn't find cloth to make a new winter coat for me. I wasn't tall, but I had gained a few centimeters over the summer, and now my coat was short in the sleeves and tight in the shoulders.

"Never mind," Maman said. "I can fix it." All in one weekend she picked apart the seams of the coat and re-sewed them. She made the coat as large as she could. It fit better then, but it looked odd. The fabric was brighter near the seams.

Papa hated working for the Germans. Etienne hated not being a soldier. Pierre disliked going to school. Maman missed our pretty house, her piano, her kitchen. Food at school was dreadful, with no meat or flour and only winter vegetables—cabbages, potatoes, rutabagas.

"Eat it," Soeur Margritte would scold me. "No one cares if you don't like it, Suzanne. Eat it, and thank God for your blessings."

How was I supposed to do that? What would I say? *Thank you, God, for not making me a Jew. Thank you for not making me a black person or anyone else that Hitler would hate. Thank you for not giving the Nazis a reason to make me disappear.*

I couldn't imagine God having much patience with such prayers. And no matter what Soeur Margritte said, I refused to be thankful for rutabagas.

Still I knelt and tried to pray. I tried to be honest and I tried to be true, and what came out was *Dear God, make me strong. Make me sing, and make me strong. Take care of my family. Make me strong.*

On my fourteenth birthday Papa gave me half a chocolate bar. "Oh, Papa!" I said. I hadn't seen so much chocolate in months, and oh, I had been wanting it for so long. With sugar rationed and so hard to find, we almost never ate anything sweet. "How did you get it?"

Papa shrugged. "I traded some cigarettes," he said.

"Oh, thank you," I said. I broke off some pieces and handed them to my brothers. Maman refused her share, and so did Papa.

"Enjoy it," he said. "You are a good girl."

I ate most of that chocolate myself. I didn't take any to school. But on Sunday afternoon I put the last square into my pocket and went to see Yvette.

She still sat and stared into nothing; she still never spoke or smiled. But she listened to her mother now when her mother told her to do something. She washed the dishes, she cleaned, she helped with laundry. She was like a mechanical person. She was dusting the parlor when I came in.

"Dear Yvette," I said, "I've brought you a treat." I had gotten into the habit of talking to her the way you might talk to a dog that you liked, kindly but without expecting an answer. I took the piece of chocolate and popped it into Yvette's mouth.

She didn't seem startled. She didn't look happy. Her mouth moved, sucking at the chocolate, and her throat muscles moved when she swallowed. Then she looked right at me. I might have imagined it, but I thought she asked a question with her eyes.

"I'm sorry," I said. "I don't have any more."

She went back to her dusting.

"I think she might have heard me," I said to her mother.

"Maybe," her mother said. "I don't hope for much anymore, but maybe you are right."

⌒

Spring came suddenly, with a hint of warmth on the wind and a bursting of flowers in the garden at school. I saw the yellow jonquils waving and thought of Maman's flowers in our garden at home, at our real home, and I felt fury well up inside me. That night after lights-out I started a pillow fight.

It wasn't entirely my fault. Odette was yammering on again, about *la belle* France and how difficult life was, about how she hated the Germans and how she couldn't have a new dress this spring because they had to use their clothing rations for her sister's First Communion dress and what a tragedy it was, and I thought, *I am so sick of Odette.* So I took my pillow and hit her on the head.

Of course she hit me back. Martine and Colette leapt from their beds and joined in. We whacked each other furiously, harder and harder. I swung my pillow sideways and knocked Martine to the floor. Colette whacked me on the backside, and I fell across Martine.

She giggled. I laughed. We scrambled up, and both of us went after Colette.

I think Odette's pillow ripped first. The convent pillows were well stuffed with feathers, but the casings were old and they tore easily. *Wham! Wham!* Soon feathers flew out of our pillows with every blow. *Wham!* Feathers floated among us like giant snowflakes. Odette grabbed a handful and threw them at me. *Wham!* My stomach hurt from laughing. It had been a year, probably, since I had laughed so hard. *Wham!* Great bursts of feathers, explosions of feathers, feathers everywhere. *Wham!*

The door opened. Soeur Margritte flipped a switch, and the lights came on full force. We stood in our nightgowns, covered in feathers. Feathers coated the floor, the beds, our hair. Dozens of feathers still whirled in the air. I was impressed. I'd never seen so many feathers. I didn't know it took that many feathers to make pillows.

Colette still had a few feathers left in her sack of a pillow. She gently shook them out. "*Pardon,* Sister," she said softly. "We became carried away."

Soeur Margritte was kind, and she looked as though she sympathized, but when she spoke, her voice was firm. "I will excuse you from your classes for half a day," she said, "during which time you will pick up every single feather. By hand."

"By hand?" Martine said, incredulously.

"By hand," said Soeur Margritte. "Not even a broom to help you. And of course you'll not be permitted home this weekend. Good night, girls." She put out the light. "Sleep well."

It was difficult to sleep with no pillow and a bed covered in feathers. My arms ached from all that whacking. I knew my parents would not be pleased when they heard of my punishment. But it had been worth it, every bit.

"Odette?" Colette whispered. "Your little sister needs a First Communion dress. It isn't her fault that there's a war."

"I know," Odette said gently. "I know."

～〽

Etienne graduated from school that spring. He had trouble finding a job, because of his injury and because there weren't many jobs to be had in wartime, but eventually he found part-time work as a shop clerk. Even that sometimes exhausted him. One day he limped home on his crutches, and when he sat down at the kitchen table his hands were trembling. Maman hurried to make him a cup of tea. Coffee we had no more, wine we had no more, but we still had tea.

"It's nothing, Maman," he said. "It'll pass. The store was busy today, and then to come home . . ."

His voice trailed off, but we knew. He had a long walk home to the cemetery apartment, and then a steep flight of stairs.

"It's too much," Maman said. "You don't need to work. We don't need you to."

"Maman." Etienne spoke carefully. "I need to work. I can't sit at home like a child. I need to be doing something." After a moment he added, "If I could go to university . . ." His voice trailed off again. All the universities and colleges were closed because of the war.

"Well," said Maman, "we can worry about that later." Her brow creased. I knew, we all knew, that she didn't want Etienne to go to college. She feared it would be too much for him. Even I could see that it might be. The monastery school had been a gentle place, and Etienne had not had to walk much while he was there.

Etienne eased himself into the front room and carefully lay down on the couch. He grimaced and closed his eyes. "Will it bother you if I practice my singing?" I asked.

"No," he said. "No, of course not. Sing away."

⟶

That summer I increased my music lessons to three times a week, again taking them at Madame Marcelle's apartment. I still sang with the church choir, and I was given a new solo to learn for the Feast of the Assumption. Sometimes I visited my friends Colette and Martine, and every week poor mute Yvette, but I also often took the bus to visit my aunt Suzanne. She and my battalion of cousins were doing well again now that winter was over; they lived out in the country and had not been much bothered by the Germans.

Once I spent the night with her. The next morning was beautifully warm. I had to get back for a singing lesson, so soon after breakfast I said good-bye to my aunt, kissed my little cousins, and set out for home. It was several miles, but I knew I could eventually flag down a bus to Cherbourg.

The grassy fields smelled fragrant and rich in the summer sunshine. The air smelled like salt even so far from the sea. My aunt had fried an egg for my breakfast. Eggs were something I didn't get to eat often anymore, and the memory of it lingered in my mouth. It was a good day to be walking. I felt wonderfully free and happy, and when I heard an engine behind me, I raised my arm to stop the bus without even looking around.

"Heil!"

I jumped. The engine was not a bus. It was a jeep filled with Nazi soldiers. I stopped where I was, but I did not say *"Heil"* back to them. I would not say that, not to Hitler or to anybody else.

The jeep continued just past me and then stopped. One of the soldiers climbed out and walked over to me leisurely. "Papers," he said.

I took my identification papers from my pocket and handed them to him. I was fourteen years old and had nothing to hide. I wasn't sure why they had stopped me. But any German soldier could stop any French person for any reason at any time. You had to have your papers ready.

My papers bore only my name, photo, and address, and a government stamp. There wasn't much to see. But the soldier studied them carefully for a long time, tilting the photo this way and that and then looking up at me to see if I matched my picture.

I waited. He cleared his throat and scratched himself. I could feel sweat starting down my back. My mouth tasted sour. The man carried my papers back to the jeep and showed them to another soldier. They spoke in German. What were they looking for?

Finally the first soldier came back to me. "Here you go," he said. "Thank you."

I put my papers back into my pocket. I didn't reply.

He indicated the jeep with a sideways nod of his head. "You want a ride? We're going to Cherbourg."

I shook my head.

He looked amused. "Can you speak?" he asked.

I nodded.

"Say 'yes,' " he said.

"Yes," I said.

"All right, then." He smiled. "Good-bye."

In French there are two words for good-bye. *Adieu* means "good-bye, I won't see you again." *Au revoir* means "see you soon." The German said "see you soon."

The jeep roared off in a cloud of dust. My knees were shaking and my stomach churned. I couldn't believe how the Germans could destroy even a peaceful morning. "No," I said. "No, you won't see me soon. *Sales Boches.*" Dirty Germans.

CHAPTER TEN

*I*n the fall of 1941 Pierre and I started our final year of school. Even though he was older we were in the same year because he had been sick for a long time as a young child. Etienne had lost a year of school too because of breaking his back. Papa said I was the strong one.

I didn't feel strong. I felt fretful and impatient and dissatisfied. I wished I could be an opera singer now. Cherbourg had a good company and they put on three or four full-stage operas every year; that fall they were doing *Tosca*. I thought I could sing better than the female lead. "Not yet," Madame Marcelle said soothingly. "You don't want to risk your career by pushing your voice now. Be patient. Attend to your studies. Next year will be soon enough to perform."

It would be forever until next year.

Maman surprised me with a new dress; I didn't know

where she had gotten the material. It was beautifully made and very grown-up, with a ruffled neckline and a short skirt. "See, here is an advantage to living in wartime," Maman said teasingly. "My mother wouldn't have permitted such a short skirt. But I didn't have enough fabric to make it longer."

Still, it was hard to be happy, even though I had always liked school. On our last morning at home Etienne looked as though he wished he could go with us. He had grown a little stronger through walking so much, but he was always in pain. I knew he longed for a better job.

Pierre was miserable because he liked summer better than school. I was caught between wanting to be done with school forever, so I could sing, and wanting the last year and a half not to have happened, so that Yvette and I could go to our first day together, hand in hand, as we used to.

I'd gone to see her the week before. She was docile and well trained; she did much around the house. "She could come to school," I said to her mother. "She wouldn't have to speak. She could write all her assignments. The sisters would understand."

"Oh, my dear Suzanne," her mother said heavily. "She can't. She won't leave the house. My dear, I know it's hard, but you must see. She isn't getting any better."

"Maybe she should go to a hospital," I said.

Madame Gireau looked frustrated, and I regretted my words. "Dr. Leclerc has come a hundred times. He says there's nothing more to do. Keep her happy, he says."

"Is this happy?"

Again I could have bitten my tongue. I shouldn't ask questions that could only hurt. Madame Gireau touched Yvette's cheek. "Oh," she said, "who can tell?"

So I was starting school again, with the same roommates and no best friend.

"Find a new best friend," Pierre said as we walked off together.

"I can't," I said. "No one else understands me."

"Find a friend who doesn't understand you," Pierre said. "Why make it so complicated?"

"I am an artist!" I said. "I need someone who understands!"

Pierre thought that was hilarious. "Oh, an artist. The great artist Suzanne David. I see. An *artist*." He doubled up laughing. I smacked him, but he laughed so hard that soon I was laughing too.

⌒ᴧ

On December 7 the Japanese bombed an American naval base in Hawaii. The Americans responded by entering the war. We were all happy. From what we had been able to learn, the war wasn't going well for France; we had nothing but German victories to endure. England's defenses had barely been enough to keep England herself from being overrun. Perhaps the Americans would be able to push the Germans out of France. Out of the whole world, eventually, but especially out of France.

"What's General de Gaulle doing now, Papa?" Etienne asked one day.

"How do I know?" Papa replied. "Do I look like a spy?"

Papa didn't look like a spy. "How would we know?" Pierre said teasingly. "If you were a good spy, we wouldn't be able to tell."

Papa laughed. "If I were a spy, I'd be a very good spy," he said. "But I'm not a spy, no. And I don't know what de Gaulle is doing. I wish I did."

I stared at Papa, hearing his words over in my mind: *if I were a spy.* I didn't think for one moment that Papa actually was a spy, but the phrase awakened a sense of possibility in me. I'd understood from the start of the war that there were people in France spying on the French for the Germans, but I hadn't considered that the opposite must be true, that there were people spying on the Germans. Fighting for the Free French. For de Gaulle.

"Do you think there are spies here?" I asked. "In Cherbourg?"

"Of course there are, ninny," Pierre said. "Don't be such a child. You must have heard of the Resistance!"

"She's an artist," cut in Etienne. My brothers were not going to let me forget what I had said. "She doesn't have to pay attention to such things."

I ignored him. "Of course I've heard of the Resistance," I said, "but spies—"

"What do you think the Resistance *is?*" said Pierre.

"Suzanne," Papa said, "this isn't something we should talk about."

I stopped talking about it. We all did. But afterward, if I was walking through the city streets and saw someone who seemed especially sad or ill or ordinary, I would think, *Perhaps that person's life isn't so bad. Perhaps that person is only pretending.*

Perhaps that person is a spy.

⌒ᴧ

The next Friday evening when I came home from school, my parents and Etienne were deep in conversation. Maman looked both frightened and excited, Papa grave, and Etienne emphatic.

"We should go, why not?" he said. "What harm could it do? At the worst they would throw us out again."

"That isn't the worst they could do," said Papa.

"But if they're not giving official permission—" Maman said at the same time.

Etienne said, "The street has been open this entire week!"

And Papa said, "The regiment isn't returning—I know that for certain."

I slid my schoolbag onto the floor and carefully shut the door behind me. I was shivering. The wind had been bitterly cold.

"Hello," my brother said. "Have you heard? The German soldiers removed the blockade from our street. The soldiers have gone. The houses have sat empty all week."

I caught my breath. "You mean we can go home?"

"That's the question," Papa said. "No one knows. No one has said that we can, no one has said that we cannot."

"Oh, please!" I said. "Let's go now!" I thought of spending Christmas in our own home. I thought of waking up in my own room instead of a closet, with my posters and pictures on the walls. Aunt Suzanne and the battalion would come for a proper Christmas dinner, a roast goose or some decent beef—we could go to midnight Mass and everything would feel right again. It would feel just as always.

Papa said, "No matter what, we should wait until tomorrow. Saturday—" Just then Pierre burst through the door.

"Our house is empty!" he said. "The Germans are gone. Hurry! Let's go!"

"Dinner," Maman said, but we didn't want dinner. Pierre and Etienne and I didn't care about anything except being home again.

"We'll just have a look around," Maman said. "We won't be able to move back tonight. We will return here to sleep. We don't know what the house will be like inside."

We barely listened. Etienne put on his coat. I rebuttoned mine and slipped my toothbrush into my pocket just in case. If everything in the house was as we had left it, we might be able to stay.

The street seemed just the same. It wasn't as tidy as it had been, but all the houses were standing just as they ought, windows, doors, roofs intact. It was quieter than it should have been, but here and there a light in a window showed that some other family had returned. Our home with its pleasant stone steps looked like a long-lost friend.

"Hmmm," Maman said under her breath. "They never trimmed the rosebushes."

Papa no longer had a key, and the front door was locked. He wrapped his hand in his coat and carefully smashed the pane of glass in the door, then reached through and turned the handle.

As he swung the door open, a horrible smell rolled toward us like a fog. We choked and spluttered. It took me a moment to realize the terrible smell was coming from inside our own house.

"Oh, *mon Dieu*," said Maman. "My God, what have they done?"

Papa reached for the hall switch. The lights came on, but we were amazed to see only bare lightbulbs hanging from a hole in the plaster ceiling. Our light fixtures were gone.

Our table was missing from the hallway. Our dining room furniture was gone, our rugs, our sideboard. The parlor was stripped bare; everything, including Maman's piano, was gone. Maman turned the parlor light on and gave a gasp. The pretty seascape mural she had had painted on the wall was ruined. It looked as if a bucket of whitewash had been thrown across it. Streaks of whitewash had run down the wall and hardened in puddles on the wood floor.

Maman touched the edge of the whitewash and then put her hand to her mouth. "Why would they do this?" she asked. "We gave them our house without protest."

"They sold our furniture," Pierre said.

"Or sent it to Germany," Papa agreed. His face looked like a mask, so set was his expression.

"But why would they ruin something that was beautiful?" Maman sounded more puzzled than anything else. I put my arm around her.

In the kitchen everything was gone but a plain table. The telephone had been ripped from the wall. In the bath the toilet was gone, and also the mirror. In the laundry we found the source of the horrible smell. The soldiers had apparently used our laundry sink as a toilet. It was clogged with human refuse. Inside the room the stench was overwhelming.

"Mon Dieu," Maman whispered again.

"I'll clean it," said Etienne through clenched teeth.

Upstairs they had left all the beds but stolen all the mattresses. They had taken or removed everything else.

Everything. I was stunned. I walked into my room, which I had thought about so often, and it was as though the room in my mind had never existed. In the middle of the bare floor my empty bedstead stood under a bare lightbulb. My dresser, rugs, curtains—gone. My clothes, books, toys—gone. My baby pictures. My dolls. I could see the places on the walls where they had torn down my poster of Tino Rossi, my movie star trading cards. Why had they taken things that meant nothing to them?

Why had they taken things that meant everything to me?

Everything gone. I walked around and around my empty room, trying to make sense of it. In the corner of the closet I saw something wedged against the wall. I pulled it out. It was a photograph of me at age seven. My dark hair was cut in a bob, and I looked very serious, but I remembered when the photograph had been taken—it had been a happy day. I took it out to show my mother.

My parents' room and the boys' room both looked like mine—the beds still there, but no mattresses, nothing else. I gave the photo to my mother. She smiled. "Look how beautiful you were," she said.

Papa said gruffly, "We are all here together. That is what counts."

"I'm glad they stole the mattresses," Pierre said. "I would not sleep where they did."

CHAPTER ELEVEN

*C*leaning the house didn't take that long, but re-furnishing it did. Papa put a list of everything that was missing into an ad in the newspaper, and some things, including a dresser, our dining room table, and our clock, were returned to us. People had bought them from the Germans not knowing where they had come from, and when they realized what they had done, they gave our things back to us. No one asked us to pay them. Other things, including our bicycles and Maman's piano, we never heard about again.

The small things—the really important things, the photographs, the books, the mementos—were gone forever. I wished I had taken my baby album from the house and left my winter coat behind.

All the houses on the street, except Dr. Leclerc's on the corner, had been occupied by Germans too, so no one had witnessed what they had done. Dr. Leclerc said he was very sorry but he had not heard or seen anything. The Germans had left him alone, but like everyone else, he had been forbidden to walk down the street and had had to approach his own house from a side alley. He had not known our furniture was gone.

We couldn't find new mattresses anywhere. Apparently no one made them during a war. Eventually Maman and Papa found an old lumpy mattress for themselves, but even by Christmas the boys and I were still sleeping on pallets on the floors of our rooms.

We had left the cemetery apartment as quickly as we could carry out all our things. We cleaned our old house, painted over the ruined mural, and fixed everything as best we could. We found some rugs and an old sofa. Madame Marcelle gave me new movie star cards to pin to my wall. Naked lightbulbs still swung from the ceilings. It was nothing like the house we had had before. Sometimes I felt like a stranger in my own home.

Christmas was not a roast goose or some beef or even a nice leg of lamb. Christmas was more fish, more mussels, some sad-looking flageolets, more rutabagas, some cabbages, and no candy at all. Not even for the battalion, not even for the little ones. My mother had saved her ration coupons in an attempt to make a feast, but there wasn't any butter or sugar to buy even for those with coupons. Aunt Suzanne arrived with wine and cigarettes, and Etienne brought out a bag of apples and gave one to each of our little cousins.

"Hey," said Pierre, "where did you get those?" We had not seen apples since summertime.

"I traded for them," Etienne said, "from a man at work."

"You might have gotten some for the rest of us," Pierre sniffed.

I would have loved to eat an apple, but I wished even more that I had thought to find something to give the others. Isabelle, my smallest cousin, brought her apple to me. "Take a bite," she said, holding it up. "It's sweet."

I took a bite. It was sweet, but the sweetness made me sad. I longed for Christmases the way they used to be, knee-deep in candy and toys. Yet the Christ child was born in a stable—nothing was very comfortable for Him, either. *Dear God,* I prayed as always, *make me strong.*

A few weeks later, on a Friday night, Papa came home with a small paper package in his arms. "See here," he called out. "Maman, you children, come see." He opened the package on the kitchen counter with great flourish.

"Beef!" Maman cried. It was good, fresh beef, one big steak, perhaps a kilo in weight. My mouth watered at the sight.

"A man I know butchered a cow," Papa said.

"Well, all right," said Maman. "Something I can cook! We'll have a pretty good dinner tonight." She looked the beef over and nodded. "Slice some rutabagas, Suzanne. Set the table, *hein?*"

Pierre went out to the shed to get a hammer. He and Papa were trying to fix one of the lights. He left the door ajar. Maman was in the pantry. I turned from the table just in time to see a large black cat dash into the kitchen. It leapt onto the counter and grabbed the entire beefsteak in its mouth. I shouted. The cat sprang off the counter and dashed out the door, dragging the steak along.

"Wretched cat!" I yelled, throwing open the door. "Stupid *beast!*"

Pierre was coming from the shed. He startled the cat, which dropped the meat and ran. Pierre picked the steak up and brought it into the house. It was covered with mud and cat hair. The cat had bitten off a large chunk.

"So, we wash it, yes?" Maman said. "It will still taste fine."

We were all angry at the cat, Pierre, Etienne, and me, and we did not get less angry after we ate what was left of the steak. It was not so appetizing to eat what a cat had chewed. Halfway through dinner Pierre elaborately removed a cat hair from his mouth. I felt slightly sick. Also the piece of steak didn't seem so very large after it was divided among the five of us. I resented the bit that the cat had eaten.

The cat came back to the door as I was washing dishes. Pierre was wiping them, and Etienne was sitting at the table. Papa and Maman were in the other room. "There's that horrid cat," I said. On the other side of the door, the cat meowed.

"Wants more beefsteak," said Etienne.

"He had plenty," I said. "He got his share."

"We should teach him to stay away from here," said Pierre. "Otherwise he'll keep coming back."

"Ha," I said. "I wonder what he'll eat next time."

"We ought to put him in the well," said Etienne.

We had an old stone well at the edge of our garden. It was shallow and had been dry for years. It had a heavy lid. "That cat deserves it," I said. "Plenty of food for cats to eat. He can catch mice."

Pierre and I looked at each other.

Etienne got up slowly. He reached for his crutches. "Just for the night," he said. "Just so he learns not to come back here, that's all."

I opened the back door and picked up the cat. He was heavy, fat, well fed. He purred. I carried him across the garden and Pierre slid the lid off the well. I dropped the cat in. Pierre replaced the lid. We could hear the cat scrambling inside and then yowling as he realized he was trapped. "Sleep well, cat," said Pierre. "See you in the morning." We walked back to the house.

Papa was at the door. "What are you doing?"

"Nothing, Papa," said Pierre.

"I saw you with that cat."

"Only to teach him to stay away—"

"You scoundrels! You wretched children!" Papa waved his arms and shouted. "Have you no sympathy? Who brought you up, that you should be so mean to a hungry animal? Where is that poor cat?"

Papa marched to the well and yanked the lid aside. The cat jumped into his arms. "Ah, yes, my poor little one," Papa said, stroking it. "Come inside. It's a hard world for cats as well as people. Pierre! Find a saucer. Fetch some milk. Our new cat needs a treat."

Pierre brought it, grumbling. I caught Etienne's eye and the two of us burst out laughing. "We didn't know you liked cats, Papa," said Etienne.

"I don't," said Papa. The cat rubbed its face against Papa's chin. "Except this one. His name is Miki, and you are never to put him in the well again."

Miki slept on Papa's bed, right against him, like a dog. Maman fed him fish heads. Papa fed him the finest bites from his own plate. After dinner he poured milk into a saucer and let Miki lap it up right on the table. Miki adored Papa. Soon he watched in the window for Papa to come home at night. Papa would wad a scrap of paper into a ball and throw it, and Miki would bring it back to him, just like a little dog.

CHAPTER TWELVE

Spring came. The war continued. I graduated from the convent school. I was fifteen; my education was finished. The universities were shut, but I would not have wanted to go anyway. All I wanted to do was sing. My practices and lessons with Madame Marcelle intensified.

One bright summer day Madame Marcelle said I was ready to perform.

"Really perform?" I asked. I had sung in the church choir for years.

"The Cherbourg opera company is producing *L'Auberge du Cheval Blanc, The Inn of the White Horse,*" said Madame Marcelle. "It's a lightweight opera, very lyrical, not too much drama," she continued. "It will be good for your first one. Auditions are next week. You must not be afraid."

"Auditions, *madame?* Can I do it? May I go? Are you certain?" I could hardly believe it. At last!

"Make sure you have a suitable dress to wear," she continued. "Perhaps I should discuss it with your mother. I'm sure she can help you find something."

"I don't know this opera. Is it a good one? Are there any good parts? Will I sing in the chorus?"

"Bah," said Madame Marcelle. "You will sing Josépha, the lead."

On the day of the audition I could not eat. Madame Marcelle walked me to the opera house. Maman had found a piece of wine-colored velveteen and hastily made me a new dress; the fabric was nothing like as nice as what we could have gotten before the war, but I knew I looked as fine as anyone else who would be there. I wore my hair curled and piled very high above my forehead, and I borrowed my mother's high-heeled shoes.

"What if they find out I'm only fifteen?" I asked.

Madame Marcelle turned to me in amazement. "What difference would that make? Goodness, Suzanne, they are going to judge you on your voice and your grace, not on your age. Besides, they know how old you are. I have been telling the director these last three years that I would send you when you were ready. He will be glad to see you."

If anything, this made me feel more nervous. Now I had to live up to the director's expectations. The opera house was large, and when I took my turn on the stage, the empty seats in front of me seemed to reach to heaven. My knees and hands trembled. My stomach flopped.

Then the music began. The instant I opened my mouth I knew I belonged onstage. For my audition Madame Marcelle had taught me one of Josépha's arias, and as I sang I began to move across the stage. I had not planned this; I always stood still when I sang with my teacher. Now as the melody poured from my throat, I walked forward toward the edge of the stage, gesturing with my hands, beckoning, beseeching, imploring. Singing, singing. I had never felt more alive. I was sorry when the music stopped; I wanted to sing forever.

The director applauded. He cast me as Josépha.

The weeks of rehearsal spun by with dizzying speed. I was the youngest singer in the cast, but we were all singers. I felt comfortable with them right away, and I thought they were comfortable with me.

It would have been grander before the war. Instead of getting new costumes, my mother made mine over from ones the company had used the previous season. Instead of an eight o'clock curtain, we performed in the late afternoon so that the audience could get home before the blackout began. The props and sets were not fancy. Still, it was opera. We gave four performances to full houses. I got a standing ovation at each one.

My brothers brought me flowers for the opening.

"Roses!" I said. "Where did you get roses?" But they wouldn't tell me.

"Not a bad performance for such a little girl," said Etienne.

"Your voice is bigger than you are," said Pierre.

Papa hugged me hard and blew his nose. "Pretty good," he said. "Pretty good." Maman said nothing, but her eyes shone, and I knew she was proud of me too.

"I guess we can't laugh at you anymore," Pierre said, shaking his head with mock regret. "I guess you really are an artist now."

⌣ᴧ

I sang, I sang, I sang. Madame Marcelle took me different places, to Bayeux and Saint-Lô. We went to concerts, we went in search of music and costumes; sometimes she took me to other instructors. The buses almost never ran on time. If we got home late at night, I slept on her sofa instead of waking my parents. They never worried when I was with Madame Marcelle.

In July the Nazis began to round up all the Jews in France. I did not know any Jews in Cherbourg; I did not see anyone disappear. But one of my uncles in Paris wrote that his neighbors had been taken. He had seen them herded into the street, marched along like sheep under the threat of German guns. My uncle had tried to intervene. "But what could I do?" he wrote. "A German soldier grabbed my arm and pushed me aside, and I knew it was a fight I could not win."

My uncle had only one arm. He had lost the other in the Great War. I knew the soldier could have shot my uncle as easily as he had pushed him aside. But I hated to think of my uncle backing down, being afraid. "My neighbors were good people," he wrote. "They were taken away on a train, in cattle cars, no one knows where."

In the fall I sang the role of Mimi in *La Bohème*. Again I danced and sang and flitted about the stage. My dress was red and rich-looking; from the audience you could not see the seams where Maman had carefully cut and shaped and sewn it together again so that the moth holes would not show.

It sometimes felt odd not to be in school. Even when I was rehearsing, I had more free time than when I had been going to school. Madame Marcelle made me sing several hours a day, but she also told me not to sing too much. "You could strain your voice if you push too hard," she said. "We want you strong. Sing well within your capabilities, and with time you will be able to do more and more."

So again I prayed, *Make me strong.*

Etienne still worked part time. Pierre got a job running messages for one of the big hotels downtown. Most of his customers were German officers. "It's not so bad," he said. "You say, 'Yes, sir, yes, sir,' and they leave you alone."

Yet one day he came home with an ugly red mark on his cheek. "What happened?" Maman said.

Pierre looked ashamed. "I had to go from the hotel to the Quai Alexandre. I went the way I would always go, Maman, I mean before the war. I just didn't think. I forgot about the restricted area." The street next to ours was still off-limits, as were some of the streets downtown.

The color drained out of Maman's face. "What did they do?"

"Only slapped me, Maman, and told me to be more careful. Said to remember to stay where I belonged."

"Then remember it," Maman said sharply. "Obey their rules and you will not be hurt."

Unless you are a Jew, I thought. *Unless their rules say that you will be hurt no matter what you do.*

I was walking home from my aunt Suzanne's house a week or so later when the Allies bombed Cherbourg. The road was dusty and the grass in the fields was high. I could see the planes far off and hear the noise of their engines. I saw the bombs falling. I began to run even before the sounds of the explosions reached my ears.

They were after the arsenal, I was sure—the great building near the harbor where submarines could dock, and where the Germans stored their ammunition. The arsenal was a treasure trove, and the Allies wanted it destroyed.

The arsenal was next to the train station, where Papa worked. I ran harder.

I could see smoke billowing up and hear sirens, but I could not tell what had been hit. *Papa*, I thought. *Papa*.

My shoes were not made for running. One of the straps around my ankles broke and flapped against the ground. I stumbled, nearly falling, but pushed on. If something horrible had happened, I needed to be there right away. If Papa needed help—

I didn't realize that a bus was behind me until it drew alongside and the driver opened the door. "Stop!" he yelled. "Where are you going?"

I recognized the driver, though I didn't know his name. "Cherbourg," I gasped, panting for breath. "They're bombing—"

"Yes, yes," the man said.

"Papa—at the depot—"

"Monsieur David?" the driver asked. I nodded. "Don't panic," he said. "He'll be all right. Get in."

I climbed onto the bus and dropped into the closest seat. I put my head in my hands. The driver turned and spoke to the other passengers. "We're just going to take a little detour," he said. "This young lady's father works near the arsenal."

You would think the other passengers would have minded being taken out of their way like that, but in war people understood. The bus driver took us straight into town. Part of the arsenal had been hit and was on fire, but the bus driver approached the train station from the other side, and I could see that it was intact, unharmed. My knees quivered with relief. I jumped off the bus and ran into Papa's office. He was standing near the window. When I threw my arms around him, he patted my head. "Suzanne, Suzanne," he said, "don't worry so. You must have courage. We will all be fine."

I supposed I lacked courage. I wasn't at all sure that we would be fine.

Dear God, make me strong. Give me some courage too.

CHAPTER THIRTEEN

On November 11 the German and Italian armies invaded Vichy France, the part of France that General Pétain governed and that the Germans had previously agreed to leave alone. We were not surprised. "You can't trust Hitler," Maman said, shaking her head.

Papa said, "At least we are back to being one France now. We are all under Germany's heel."

⌒ᴧ

In the spring of 1943 I was carrying a knife across the kitchen when I slipped. I caught myself on the counter, but the end of the knife cut through my blouse and into my shoulder just above my left breast. It was a small cut, but it became infected.

The Germans had taken all our medicines, of course; it was now impossible to buy even an aspirin. Maman tried to draw the infection out with hot compresses, but it grew worse. The area swelled, and the skin became shiny and red. It felt hot and hard.

"Does it hurt?" Maman asked me, pressing the compress gently against my skin. I bit my lip and nodded. "Well, I don't know," she said. She sat back and looked at me. Lines of worry etched her face. "I suppose we wait. It may get better."

I trudged off to my music lesson. My whole body felt feverish, and my head hurt. When I opened the door of Madame Marcelle's apartment, she came toward me with her hands held out. "Suzanne, good news!" she cried. "The company's next opera will be *Carmen*! *Carmen*!"

Carmen is a great tragedy, one of the best operas ever written. The music is superb. You can bet I wanted to get that lead. In an instant I forgot my discomfort. "Oh, *madame*!" I said. "Am I ready?" I had always dreamed of singing Carmen.

"You will be," she said. "Come, we have so much work to do."

Madame and I stepped up the intensity of my lessons. I sang for hours every day. I practiced over and over. When I won the role of Carmen I sang even more.

"We shouldn't have to go see her onstage," Pierre grumbled. "We're hearing the entire opera every day."

"*Tais-toi!*" I said. "Be quiet! You're not hearing all of it, only my part."

"Oh," said Etienne with mock surprise, "are there other parts beyond yours?"

"Remember," Pierre said gravely, "she's an artist."

Meanwhile Maman's compresses did nothing to cure the infection in my shoulder. It gradually grew worse until it hurt even to move my arm.

"Maman," I said, "I can't sing Carmen with my elbow pinned to my side."

Maman sighed. "We had better go see Dr. Leclerc," she said, "though Lord knows what he can do in that empty office of his." Dr. Leclerc didn't have medicines either.

Maman went with me. Dr. Leclerc's office was attached to his house, on the ground floor; we entered it off the street.

"Bonjour, *madame, mademoiselle*," he said as we went in. He stood up from his desk, and he shook Maman's hand and smiled at us both. I saw that his smile didn't reach his eyes. He looked old and worn, much more so than the last time I'd seen him. Perhaps he was only tired. He worked hard, I knew, despite his lack of supplies. I saw him walking down the street at all hours of the day and night.

In his examining room Dr. Leclerc pressed his fingers gently around the red area of infection. Pain shot across my shoulder and chest. I did not wince.

"Doesn't that hurt?" he asked, looking up.

"Very much," I said.

"And here?"

"Even more."

He nodded. "I remember," he said. "You're a tough one. I'm glad, because you have quite an abscess there. I will need to drain it—with a knife, you understand— and I have nothing with which to deaden the pain."

"I understand," I said.

Maman shook her head. "Poor child," she whispered.

Dr. Leclerc went into the front room and returned with a small glass bottle. "This much whisky I have hidden from the Germans," he said. He poured half of it into a small cup. "Drink it. It may help some." Then he smiled. "And when we have finished, perhaps your mother and I will drink the rest."

The whisky felt like fire going down. Dr. Leclerc cleaned my side with soap and water. He laid out a tray with his scalpels and with needle and thread. "If I were you, I would close my eyes," he said. "Scream all you wish, but try not to thrash too much. *Madame*, perhaps you will hold down her hands."

"She does not need to," I said. "I'll be still."

Maman looked sad. "I would like to hold your hand, *ma chère*," she said.

So Maman held my hand lightly, I looked up at the ceiling, and Dr. Leclerc put a knife into my shoulder.

The pain was worse than I thought it could be, much worse than the pain of the abscess itself. I didn't cry out. I held still.

Dr. Leclerc drained the abscess and cleaned it, then stitched up the wound. "This will heal slowly," he said. "Come back in ten days to have the stitches removed."

"In ten days I'm going to Saint-Lô," I said. "Madame Marcelle has arranged a special music lesson for me. I'm rehearsing to sing *Carmen,* you know."

"Come early in the day, then," he said. "Come before you leave." He looked at me curiously. "Do you travel much, a young girl like you?"

Maman rolled her eyes. "She's never at home these days. Rehearsals, costume fittings, special lessons—she is always going somewhere."

"You don't mind?" asked Dr. Leclerc.

"Of course not," I said. "I love singing. I love performing. I don't mind traveling at all."

⌒

Madame Marcelle went with me to have my stitches out, because we were on the way to the bus station to go to Saint-Lô. This time when we entered his office, Dr. Leclerc seemed livelier, almost happy. "Here's my tough girl," he said. "How is your singing?"

I was pleased to be a tough girl. I sang him a few bars

of *Carmen,* and he smiled at me. "Where do you travel for your singing?" he asked.

"Only in Normandy," I said. "Someday I'll sing in Paris and Brussels. Someday I'll sing all over the world."

"Someday, when this war is over," he said softly.

"Yes," I said.

Dr. Leclerc glanced at Madame Marcelle, who was sitting near the window, looking out. "Your chaperone goes everywhere with you?" he asked.

"When I'm singing," I answered. "She's my teacher, and besides, I can't go all the way to Saint-Lô alone."

"Just so," he said. He seemed to be thinking of something. "Come, let us take these stitches out."

My wound was healing, only slightly red now and only slightly painful. The stitches seemed to have grown into my skin, however, and removing them hurt quite a lot. Again I didn't wince or cry.

"Tough girl," the doctor repeated approvingly. He looked again toward the other room, where Madame Marcelle waited, and then back at me. He lowered his voice. "I could use a tough girl to do some work for me. Do you want to hear about it?"

Something in his voice chilled me. It was the Resistance. I am not sure how, but I knew it right away. As I stared at the floor, fear and hope welled up inside me and my throat slowly went dry. Goose bumps rose on my arms.

"Are you a spy?" I whispered. Dr. Leclerc, whom I had known all my life! He looked back at me steadily, silently. I realized that even the little bit he had already said endangered him. I was pleased he trusted me. I smiled. Then I thought suddenly of Madame Montagne and the helplessness I had felt the day she died in the square. I licked my lips to wet them. "Is it about the Germans?" I asked.

"You can't tell anyone," Dr. Leclerc said. "Not your mother, not your brothers, not your best friend. And if you agree to help me, you can never back out. Not ever, no matter what. You must help me until the very end."

"Is it about the Germans?" I repeated.

"It is about freedom," he said.

I lifted my chin. "I hate the Germans," I said.

His eyes looked steadily into mine. "It's about that too."

My hands began to shake. I thought of my favorite prayer—*dear God, make me strong*—and as I prayed, I felt an icy calm wash over me. At least for that moment I wasn't afraid. "Madame Marcelle will have to know," I said. "She goes everywhere with me; I couldn't hide things from her well enough. But she is safe. She has no family. She has no one to tell secrets to."

Dr. Leclerc nodded. "Come back when you return from Saint-Lô. There's a little problem with those stitches that needs to be attended to."

"They seemed fine," I said.

"There's a little problem," he said. "Nothing serious. Come back when you return."

"Oh," I said. "Oh, yes." I understood. There was no problem with my stitches; it was the lie I was supposed to use. I guessed he would tell me more about my duties then. When I left Dr. Leclerc's office, I felt at once older and younger. I was part of the Resistance! A girl like me!

What on earth would I be asked to do?

CHAPTER FOURTEEN

I didn't tell Madame Marcelle anything on the trip to Saint-Lô. I couldn't think how to begin. *I am doing something for Dr. Leclerc that may be illegal, and the Germans could hang me for it—in fact, they probably would if they caught me—but I don't know what it is. Perhaps I am a spy—what do you think?*

Perhaps I was letting my imagination run wild. Perhaps I wasn't a spy; perhaps it was nothing. Perhaps Dr. Leclerc wanted me to baby-sit or to help with paperwork in his office.

You can't tell anyone. Not your mother, not your brothers, not your best friend. And if you agree to help me, you can never back out. You must help me until the very end.

It wasn't nothing. It was spy work. *Dear God, make me strong.*

"Dr. Leclerc needs to see me," I said to Maman the next morning.

Maman was scrubbing the sink. She glanced over her shoulder. "Everything's healing?"

"Oh, yes. Only he wanted to check the stitches again."

"All right. See you later."

It was that easy.

I went alone to Dr. Leclerc's office. He was sitting at his desk, his forehead furrowed in concentration. "Suzanne," he said when he saw me. "Sit. Shut the door." He wasn't smiling. I wondered if I had done something wrong. What could it have been? I hadn't spoken to anyone, not even Madame Marcelle.

Dr. Leclerc tapped his desk with his fingers. "First of all, I'm never going to tell you more than the least you need to know," he said. "Try not to ask questions. If you must ask questions, ask them only of me. Trust no one else. No one.

"I receive messages, and I send them. I need you to carry them. You'll pick them up from me and give them to someone else. I'll tell you when and where."

"What kind of messages?" I asked.

"It doesn't matter."

"Where do you get them?"

"It doesn't matter."

"Whom do you give them to?"

"These are unnecessary questions, Suzanne."

He still had not smiled. He seemed almost angry. Where was the kind doctor I was used to?

"Are you frightened?" he asked.

I nodded slowly.

"You should be," he said. "You could be caught. I would say it is very likely that you will be caught. Perhaps your youth will shield you from suspicion. I hope so. If the Nazis catch you, they won't let you go."

My mouth had dried up. I swallowed hard.

"If you aren't brave enough, it is better that you say so now," he continued. "If you lose heart later, you will endanger others besides yourself. You will endanger me, my family, and many people you don't know. Do you think you have enough courage?"

"These messages," I said, "will they help France win the war?"

"They will increase our chances," he said.

"I have enough courage," I said.

"You are certain?"

"I am."

"All right, then." He hitched his chair closer to his desk and folded his hands. "I receive messages from the Allies for many different people. You will pass them on. When I need you, I'll send for you. You'll come to me as a patient. Perhaps this incision of yours won't heal quickly. I suggest that you may continue to have pain when you move your arm.

"When you come, I'll give you the message on a small piece of paper. You'll hide that paper on your person. Don't bother trying to read the message; it'll be written in code. You will go where I tell you and give the message to the person you meet there. You'll do it so no one sees. You will do everything as naturally as possible. Do you understand?"

I understood that it would be difficult. "How will I know whom to meet?" I asked. "Will I recognize them? Will I know their names?"

Dr. Leclerc shook his head. "Names are dangerous," he said. "You'll never know anyone's name except mine, which you already knew. You'll know the others by their numbers."

"Their numbers?" I felt slightly hysterical. "What numbers?"

"Everyone has a number," he said. He stood up and held out his hand. I shook it, feeling somewhat dazed. "You're number twenty-two. The twenty-second spy in Cherbourg. Welcome, Suzanne."

⌒ᴧ

It was hard to sleep that night. I lay on my lumpy secondhand mattress and watched the night shadows play across the ceiling. I was singing the role of Carmen at age sixteen. This seemed unreal enough. That I was now also a spy seemed incredible. Unfathomable. What would I do? Was I brave enough? Could I be a spy?

My number was twenty-two. I tried to imagine tiptoeing into a dark alley in the dead of night, whispering "twenty-two" to an old man in a tightly wrapped cloak, his face obscured, a fellow spy. I tried to picture myself sliding a piece of paper stealthily into his hand.

Then I pictured a sudden burst of light, men with flashlights swarming into the alley, Nazi soldiers wearing swastikas and crying *"Halt!"* Would they shoot me immediately, or would they torture me first, trying to find out everything I knew? Would I betray Dr. Leclerc? Could I go silent to my grave?

I pictured the cemetery as it had looked from our bleak apartment, a new plot freshly dug. Or would the Nazis take my body away instead of burying it? Would Maman and Papa ever learn of my fate?

All these horrible thoughts swirled in my head while behind them a full mental orchestra played the score for *Carmen. Quand je vous aimerai? Ma foi, je ne sais pas. Peut-être jamais! Peut-être demain!* When will I love you? My faith, I do not know! Perhaps never! Perhaps tomorrow! No wonder I couldn't sleep.

At the end of our next lesson I steeled myself to tell Madame Marcelle. *Now,* I thought. I didn't know when the doctor would call on me. I needed to be ready. I gathered the music in my hands and turned to face my teacher. "Sometimes I might carry messages," I began in a rush. "I—"

Madame Marcelle held up her hand. Her face went still. "Don't tell me any more," she said.

"But I—"

"No," she said. "You've said enough."

"But I haven't said anything yet," I said. "I need to tell you—"

Madame Marcelle shook her head and came to sit beside me. She put her hand in mine. "When you tell a lie," she said in a very conversational tone, as though we were discussing music theory, "first, say as little as possible. If you do something without explanation, it's less suspicious than if your explanation makes no sense. Second, always be as truthful as possible. Keep all the details absolutely true, except for the little central part that can't escape being a lie. The more truth you can put into the lie, the less likely it is that you'll trip yourself."

"I wasn't lying," I said.

"No," she agreed. "But you will be. Say nothing further. I'll see you tomorrow for your lesson. Practice your scales and be ready."

CHAPTER FIFTEEN

*T*he next Tuesday when I came home from rehearsal, Maman said, "Dr. Leclerc called. He wants you to stop by sometime tomorrow morning."

Papa looked up from his paper. "That shoulder still bothering you?"

"A little," I said. "Nothing too bad." Oh, my heart was beating fast.

⌒ʌ

In his inner office Dr. Leclerc peeled back the collar of my dress just enough to check the scar. While he did this, he spoke in a low tone, very rapidly. "Tonight you must go to the café by the theater at six P.M." He gave me the address. I knew it; I had been there before. "You'll get a coffee and walk toward the tables. An older woman will jump up to greet you. When she kisses you, give her this." He pressed a folded square of paper into my hand. "Her number is seven. She'll tell it to you. Tell her yours."

"I understand," I said. I felt dizzy. I started to slip the paper into my handbag.

"No, no," scolded Dr. Leclerc. "What are you thinking? You must hide it. It can't fall into the wrong hands. Do not put it in your purse or your pocket. Do not put it down at home. Keep it with you always, and keep it somewhere no one will find it, not even if they're looking for it."

I wore my hair piled very high at the front, and pinned. I thought for a moment, then reached into the mass of hair and took out one of the pins. I lifted my hair, slid the paper in, and pinned the hair back on top. I fluffed my hair out further.

"That's better," Dr. Leclerc said. "That doesn't show. Pin it down a little harder, perhaps. Remember too that you'll have to be ready to hand it over when you go into the café. At that point you can't be fumbling with your hair."

I tried to imagine how I would do it: take the message out where no one could see me, hold it in my hand, give it to number seven. *Mary, Mother of God,* I prayed, *you will have to help me. Give me strength.*

"Good," Dr. Leclerc said briskly. "Go on, then. I expect more patients soon."

Patients? I thought. *Or spies?* I didn't say anything,

but my thoughts must have shown on my face. "Remember," he said very quietly, "always remember: If you, who look like a schoolgirl, can be a spy, then anyone can be. Not just for France, but for Germany too. You can't trust anyone, not anyone at all."

"I'll remember," I said. I patted my hair once more, straightened my collar, and followed Dr. Leclerc out the examining room door. A young woman with a small, sickly-looking baby sat in the waiting room. *Patient?* I thought. *Or spy?*

⌒〜

I had rehearsal at the theater scheduled until six, but I left a few minutes early. Remembering Madame Marcelle's advice, I didn't give an excuse. "I have to go," I said, picking up my handbag and waving to the director. On the way out I stopped in the ladies' room. It was empty. I sat on the toilet and took the message out of my hair. I unfolded it. The thin handwritten letters looked like this: *XTZOM YVHJR ZDVGG TYPHL.* A code, then. Something I couldn't understand. Good. I couldn't be responsible for what the message contained; I could never give the information away. I refolded the tiny paper and tucked it inside my glove.

My heart hammered. The evening sun filled the

streets with golden light, but every person I passed looked like a Nazi to me. I felt sure everyone could see my nervousness. Everyone must suspect me. My hands were moist. A cold sweat broke out on my arms. I tried very hard not to look around as I walked toward the café. But no—I shouldn't look only straight ahead. That might seem suspicious.

What would I do if I were going to the café for coffee? Would I walk this fast? Would I walk faster? Slower? Would I seem eager to meet my unknown friend, this number seven? Should it look as though we had planned to meet, or should it look like an accident?

How was I going to get that message out of my glove? What a foolish place to put it!

Relax, I thought. *Be strong. Don't panic.*

Then I had a thought that saved me. I would pretend I was onstage. I would be an artist.

I would walk at my usual speed. I wouldn't be planning to meet anyone. I was simply an opera singer, finished with rehearsal and thirsty for a little of the vile, burnt-tasting, stagnant liquid that the cafés served now that real coffee had become more precious than gold. Yes, I was terribly thirsty. I swung my purse and whistled an aria. I walked with jaunty confidence.

I felt terrified. I was an actress and the café was my

stage. It was crowded when I went in. *Good,* I thought. *Crowded is good.* People weren't as likely to notice details in a crowd.

I ordered coffee. I opened my handbag to get money to pay for it. As I removed the money from my wallet, I slid the message out of my glove. I did it slowly, smoothly. The clerk never noticed. I gave her the money and took back my change, then picked up the hot cup of coffee. I held the message between the cup and my hand.

Where to go now? What to do? I hesitated, then felt panicky again. Surely I looked obvious—surely I looked like a spy.

Keep all the details true, I thought, *except for the inescapable lie.* So I was alone, had stopped for coffee—I should find an empty table and sit there. I scanned the crowd, not looking at faces—I wouldn't be looking at faces—but at tables. I found one and began to move toward it.

Right beside me a woman's voice shouted, "Hello!" I nearly spilled my coffee on her head.

"Marvelous, my dear, marvelous to see you!" she shouted. She was old and poorly dressed. She wore layers of faded clothes and an old felt hat. "How is your dear mother?"

This woman, this spy, didn't seem afraid of attracting

attention at all. I followed her lead. "Dear *madame*!" I cried in a tone of happy surprise. The woman threw her arms around me. We kissed, one cheek, then the other. "Seven," she whispered as she kissed my cheek.

"Twenty-two," I whispered, kissing hers.

Our enthusiastic embrace knocked some of the coffee out of my cup. She caught my hand, laughing, and took the cup from me in the most natural way. She used her handkerchief to help me wipe up. The message was in her pocket with her handkerchief before anyone could have seen.

"Sit, sit," she said. "You have to tell me—" Outside, a nearby church bell tolled the hour. "Six o'clock!" she said. "So late! What a pity! I must fly! Give my love to your mother—how nice to see you again!"

Spy number seven grabbed up a giant marketing bag and shuffled out the door. I sat alone drinking horrible coffee, with no message and a feeling of unutterable relief.

At home Maman said, "How was practice?"

"Wonderful!" I said. "I love *Carmen*." I danced around the kitchen table, singing my opening aria. "I got a coffee on the way home. It tasted like boiled pencil shavings."

"Bah!" said Maman. "The junk they sell these days! A waste of money."

That was all I said; all I could say. But that night I was kept awake by feelings of victory, not fear. I had helped the Allies. I had hindered the Germans. I was fighting for France.

CHAPTER SIXTEEN

Carmen was a triumph. The few notes that I missed, I missed with brio, with flair. The newspaper review called me "enchanting." An unknown admirer sent me flowers backstage. So did my brothers, my father, my friends.

I sang the third performance with a message pinned in my hair. On the outside I was lively, mysterious, enchanting. On the inside I was petrified.

"That was your best performance yet," Maman said when it was over.

"Oh, thank you!" I said. "Can we celebrate? I feel like celebrating. Can we go to a restaurant? Just for a drink and a snack?"

"Eh bien," said Papa. "Acting the movie star, are you? You feel you deserve to go to a restaurant?" He was teasing. He was proud of me.

"She isn't a movie star," said Pierre. "She's—"

"An artist," I said. "Yes, Pierre, I know. That joke is growing thin."

"I wasn't going to say 'an artist.' I was going to say 'a terrible glutton.' "

"Just because I'm hungry—"

"Bah," said Maman. "I'd be hungry too if I did all that running around onstage. Where would you like to go?"

I told them. We went, sat down, and ordered dessert. I excused myself to wash my hands and had just gotten back when a man stopped at our table.

"I just came from the theater," he said. "In my lifetime I have seen *Carmen* six times—*six*—and this one was the best. Such beautiful singing! Such a talented girl! Please allow me to shake your hand."

I was to meet number six. We shook, and the message I had pulled out of my hair in the washroom changed hands.

⌒〜

Summer passed, hot and stuffy. I longed for a new opera. I was eager for autumn. I carried only a few messages for Dr. Leclerc. Sometimes weeks would go by without one, and I would begin to worry that he no longer trusted me. Then several would come rapid-fire, more than one a day, and I would worry that I couldn't keep all my activities concealed.

"Suzanne?" Maman said. "Why did the doctor call again?"

"I've been having headaches." This was true. Carrying messages made my head hurt.

"Meet a woman, number thirteen, in the church of La Trinité on Wednesday at ten A.M." I cut my singing lesson short and walked to the church. I dipped my hand in the holy water, crossed myself, then clasped my hands together (the message tight between them) as though in prayer. There were two women praying in the pews. Which one? I could not kneel and whisper "twenty-two" to a housewife or a German spy. Which was the right woman? Both knelt devoutly, heads bowed. Of course I did not know what Thirteen was supposed to look like.

I walked halfway up the aisle toward the two women. I genuflected and knelt at the end of the pew, next to the aisle. The two women prayed and prayed. They didn't move. Certainly one was waiting for a message. The other, I supposed, was waiting for the answer to her prayer. *Dear God,* I prayed, *please make one of these women go away.*

I pulled my handkerchief from my pocket and wiped my nose. I started to slide the handkerchief back but let it miss my pocket and flutter to the floor while I prayed hard, eyes closed, and didn't seem to notice. Ahead of me a woman got up, genuflected unsteadily, and came down the aisle with eyes downcast. She looked as though she had been weeping. I wondered what sorrow she had known. *Good,* I thought. *It must be the other one.*

The first woman walked three steps past me, then turned slowly and came back. She bent to pick up my handkerchief. "You dropped this," she said.

"Thank you," I answered, taking it from her. *Please go away,* I thought, *so I can hand over this message and get out of here.*

"Tell your troubles to God," she said softly. "The Lord is our shepherd, we shall not want. He makes us lie down in green pastures. He leads us beside still waters. He refreshes our souls. Thirteen."

For an instant I thought she was telling me the number of the psalm she was quoting. "No, twenty-three," I corrected her automatically. Then, catching myself, almost in horror, I said, "I mean, *twenty-two.*"

"Yes." She lifted a gentle hand to my face, and for a moment I gazed into her tear-filled eyes. "The Lord protects and keeps us." She touched my fingers gently as she turned away.

That was a good one, I thought, bowing my head as she shuffled away. St. Joseph himself wouldn't have noticed that message pass between us.

That winter was miserable. The opera company sang *Le Nozze di Figaro, The Marriage of Figaro,* but even Mozart's wonderful Susanna failed to lift my spirits. We sang *Otello,* a gloomy story even for an opera. As Desdemona, I died at the end.

"You are always dying at the end," said Pierre. "Aren't you getting tired of it? Can't you play a part that ends happily?"

"It's opera," I said. "The good parts are always sad."

But I could have used some happiness, even if only onstage. Gray clouds hung in the sky, and the wind blew wet and cold day after day. We were all so tired of rationing and shortages. We were all so tired of war. I was too old now to complain about our constant diet of rutabagas and fish, but I wasn't too old to hate it.

The messages continued. Sometimes I was pleased to have something to do. Other times it frightened me. Once I gave a message to a man right under the gaze of a German guard. My heart beat so fast, I thought it might fly out of my chest. Some nights, after delivering messages, nightmares jerked me awake. I tried never to scream.

Papa worried over my headaches. "Perhaps you're singing too much."

"Oh, Papa. My head never hurts when I sing."

"Perhaps you need eyeglasses."

"Perhaps. When the war is over."

"Perhaps she needs some laughter," said Etienne. "Some parties, some good friends, a little fun."

Now that I was finished with school I rarely saw Colette or my other friends. I could have, I knew, and Maman urged me to visit them. It was hard to know what to say to them when I did. They didn't understand my singing career; they didn't understand why I took it so seriously, why I practiced all the time. And I could never tell them about my messages. Once I arranged to meet Martine for coffee only to be sent somewhere with a message at the same time. I called Martine to cancel our meeting. An hour later, when we were supposed to be having coffee, I ran into her on the street. She was hurt, and I had no way to explain.

I went to Yvette's house twice a month, on Saturday afternoons, for two hours. Her mother liked to do a little shopping then, and it gave her a chance to leave Yvette without worrying. As time went on Yvette seemed less and less human. She was always dressed and clean, and she went about her chores dutifully, but she never showed any emotion. I came to dread being with her. I went only for the sake of her mother.

I grew taller. My clothes didn't fit. Papa made good money, as the Germans had left his salary the same, and Pierre and Etienne were both working, and I was paid for my singing performances, but there was nothing to buy. I couldn't find a new dress, and it was so hard to get enough cloth to make anything new. Maman fretted over my short coat sleeves. "If I could find any decent wool at all . . . ," she murmured.

"Don't worry, Maman," I said. "I don't mind." But on the street I tugged at the sleeves, wishing the cuffs of my dress didn't show.

Just after Christmas Pierre developed a bad cough and had to stay home from work for a week. When I came home from delivering a message, he complained about my absence. "You flit around so much," he said. "You just leave without saying anything. You don't keep a schedule. Do you have a boyfriend?"

"Of course I don't have a boyfriend," I said. "What a stupid thing to say. I have a career."

"Oh, la, Miss Opera Singer," he replied with a rude wave of his hand.

"Don't fuss at me," I said, "just because I wasn't here to play chess when you wanted." I could see how poorly he felt, feverish and flushed. I didn't say anything more.

But I lay awake that night. Did Pierre really think I was gone too much? Did Maman and Papa wonder? Should I make more excuses when I left the house, or was it best to continue to say nothing?

And what about the Nazis? Did they notice my

comings and goings? Did they suspect me at all? I watched the night shadows crisscross my ceiling. I tossed and turned. My stomach hurt, and my head did too.

⁓

German soldiers still occupied the street behind ours. They walked past our house daily. I tried not to see them; I avoided looking at them even when I had to show them my papers, which was often. Sometimes one of the younger ones would call out to me or whistle. I always pretended not to hear. "Stay out of their way," Maman said, and Papa would repeat, "Do what you are told and you won't get hurt."

Meet number twelve at the Place Napoléon, in front of the statue, at noon. This was what I was told. I tried to tell myself that if I did it right, I couldn't be hurt, but I knew better.

CHAPTER SEVENTEEN

One day in early spring Madame Marcelle and I went to Saint-Lô to see about borrowing some costumes for me for the company's latest performance, *Il Barbiere di Siviglia, The Barber of Seville*. Maman had made Carmen's costumes over for Susanna, and Susanna's over for Desdemona; we could not see how she could possibly make them over again for Rosina, my new role. The theater manager in Saint-Lô was polite but would not loan us a thing. "We need our costumes for ourselves," he said. "Anyhow, moths have gotten into them. We have nothing you would want."

"How does he know?" I sniffed as we headed toward the bus stop. "I would take just about anything to avoid walking onstage in that yellow baize again."

"The baize is beyond redemption," Madame Marcelle agreed. "It can be used for a servant girl in the chorus, to show how desperate and poverty-stricken her station is." She sighed. "Perhaps we can find someone who would be willing to sell an old wedding dress. At least that would give us enough material that your mother would have something to work with."

"We could dye it," I agreed.

We reached the bus stop and fell into a discussion of the perfect costumes for Rosina as we waited for the bus to Cherbourg.

It didn't come. We waited one hour, then two. Because of the war, the buses were often off schedule. The spring breeze was chilly and we had begun to be uncomfortably cold; also, it was getting late. Finally a bus trundled by and I flagged it down.

"Going to Cherbourg?" I asked.

"I can get you almost there," the driver said. He named a crossroad just outside town.

I looked at Madame Marcelle. She shrugged. "Close enough," I said, and we climbed on.

When I was getting the bus fare from my purse, I realized something that chilled my blood. *"Madame,"* I whispered, "I left my identification papers at home."

"Suzanne!" she said. "How could you?"

It was beyond stupid, I knew. "I borrowed this purse from Maman because I was sorting through all my things. I was in a hurry. I'm sorry." Any trouble for me could be trouble for her.

Madame Marcelle shrugged. "It's not likely to matter. And it's not as though you're carrying . . ."

She let her voice trail off. I bit my lip and looked out the window. I was carrying a message in my hair. I had to hand it over that night.

Madame Marcelle took a deep breath and blew it out again. "Well. We'll be careful, that's all."

It was dusk by the time the bus let us off. I climbed down the steps and started to wave a thank-you to the driver. Madame Marcelle poked me hard in the back, and I froze.

A pack of Nazi soldiers was holding up traffic just ahead. There must have been an accident of some sort at the intersection; a German jeep was in a ditch. Half a dozen soldiers swarmed around it, their guns slung across their backs.

They hadn't noticed us yet. The bus wheezed and started to pull away. I grabbed Madame Marcelle's arm and we ducked behind the only thing near the road that would shelter us—a farmer's ancient haystack, taller than us and nearly as wide as a house. We leaned against it, out of sight.

"Do you think they'll check us if we try to walk past?" I asked.

"Are you crazy?" Madame Marcelle whispered. "What do you think?"

I knew she was right. German soldiers with time on their hands were bound to make trouble for civilians. And if they discovered I didn't have papers, certainly they'd take me in for questioning. They could easily search me then and find the message in my hair.

The Germans might suspect me already; I knew that. As time went on Dr. Leclerc looked more and more careworn. I had always believed that the messages he gave me were important. I knew also that the more important they were, the more danger I was in. I tried hard not to ask him questions, but one day I had blurted out, "Does General de Gaulle know who I am?"

For once Dr. Leclerc answered. He gave me a long level look and said, "Yes, Suzanne. He knows your name, and he has your photo."

A shiver ran up my spine. "What do you mean, he has my photo?"

Dr. Leclerc smiled grimly. "A copy of your identification photo. It wasn't hard to get. It's better to have records, Suzanne, in case a situation arises in which someone can come to your defense."

"You mean if I'm caught?"

"Just so."

"Has anyone—" A look from Dr. Leclerc made me stop before I finished my question. I supposed it was better that I not ask it. If the great General de

Gaulle, the hope of France, knew of me, then I couldn't even pretend it was a game I was playing. It was real. Deadly real.

And one evening a few weeks past, Pierre had come home from his job and said, "The Germans took old Ventreaux to Saint-Lô. They said he was a spy."

I was alarmed. "Who is old Ventreaux?"

"Just an old man," said Pierre. "He shined shoes at the hotel. He was bent over. He couldn't do much work." Pierre saw my face and added gently, "Don't worry, sister. I'm sure it isn't true. How could an old man like that be a spy?"

Papa set a saucer of milk on the floor for Miki and whistled. The cat came running. "Monsieur Edouard Ventreaux?" Papa asked.

Pierre shrugged. "I don't know his first name."

"Because Monsieur Edouard Ventreaux is retired from the navy. He's a very intelligent man."

I thought of an old man I had given messages to twice. Number four. Once he did seem hunchbacked. The other time he walked more upright. Both times he wore a navy cap.

Pierre shrugged uncomfortably. "I don't know, Papa," he said. "Monsieur Ventreaux from the hotel is gone. Should I ask where he went?"

Papa shook his head. "No. You should not."

"Did Monsieur Ventreaux have a number?" I asked Dr. Leclerc the next time I saw him.

He didn't look up. He studied something on his desk. A long silent moment passed. "Be careful, Suzanne," he said.

⁓

So now I pulled Madame Marcelle behind the haystack and tried not to think of the message in my hair.

"Mon Dieu," she muttered.

I peeked around the stack. A young boy walked past the soldiers. He stared at the jeep. One of the Germans spoke sharply to him. Another stopped the boy and held out his hand. The boy pulled his papers out of his jacket pocket and handed them over. The soldier checked them and waved the boy on. I sank back against the hay, my heart hammering.

"We'd best stay out of sight," Madame Marcelle murmured. After a few more minutes she looked carefully around the edge of the haystack. "Still there. And now they are lighting cigarettes, the fiends."

We waited. My heart gradually slowed to normal speed. I held my head carefully. When I had pinned my hair up that morning, the braids coiled round and round my head, it had seemed fine to slip the folded message into the pouf of hair in front, as I usually did. Now it seemed especially stupid. If the Germans decided to search me, of course they would take down my hair. I would. It was an obvious place! What an idiot I was.

My heart began to race again. Now I was thirsty. We didn't have food or water with us. We had expected to be home before now.

I closed my eyes and tried to breathe slowly. Birds chirped in the trees. The tall grass prickled my legs. The haystack looked slippery, gray with age. Madame Marcelle checked again. "Still there," she said. "Only two of them now. They must be waiting for someone to come for the jeep."

I knew they would never leave the jeep. I didn't blame them. If I saw a German jeep unattended in a ditch, at the very least I would grab a handful of wires out of its engine as I went past, or slit the tires if I had a knife.

Hours passed as we stood and then sat behind the stack. We grew thirstier, and hungry and cold. The sky darkened into night. When I got up to look at the Germans, my legs were stiff. I had goose bumps on my arms. "Still there," I told Madame Marcelle. I shivered.

My teacher looked wretched. "I believe we must climb into the hay," she said. "It looks as if we are here for the night. I don't wish to freeze to death."

The hay was dank. As we dug into the side of the stack, the powdery smell of mold rose around us. We dug a hole just big enough for our bodies and thrust our legs deep into the stack. The hay scratched me. Blades of it pierced my sweater. I shoved my skirt down and pulled my purse in beside me, then helped Madame Marcelle reach hers. We packed hay around us. We plugged the front of the hole near our heads loosely so that we could still breathe. All the time I tried to be careful not to dislodge the pins in my hair. I would never hide a message in my hair again.

At least we were warmer now, and lying down. "Good night, *madame*," I whispered.

"Good night, Suzanne," she whispered back. "Imagine, at my age, sleeping in a haystack."

"I'm sorry," I said. "I wish you didn't have to." If not for my carelessness, she would have been home safe in her apartment, sleeping in her bed.

"Never mind," she said. "We will call it an adventure. They say adventures keep you young."

"I am young enough already," I said.

Madame Marcelle leaned against me. "We are fine," she said. "We are safe."

I didn't feel safe, sleeping in a moldy old haystack. But the Germans had not caught me yet. I said my prayers inside my head, closed my eyes, and wished for sleep.

In the morning when we climbed stiffly out into the cold air, the Germans and their jeep were gone. Madame Marcelle brushed the hay from her skirt and gripped her handbag firmly. "Where does this message—"

"Shhh," I said.

"Mmm. Where do you go this morning, my child?"

I thought hard. I should have been at the café near the theater by five o'clock the previous afternoon. "This morning I go home," I said. "Perhaps this afternoon I should have a special lesson at the theater around five-thirty."

"That would be an excellent idea," said Madame Marcelle. "You need much practice before next week's opening, and we haven't had time to adequately rehearse your movements onstage. Pray tell your parents I am sorry to make you go so late, but it's the only time the stage is available. I won't keep you long and will have you home before dark."

"*Merci, madame,*" I said.

We went to Madame Marcelle's flat, and I sponged the dirt from my arms and legs. She picked the hay from my clothing, and I brushed it out of my hair. I put the message on the table. Madame Marcelle ignored it. She gave me a piece of bread and some tea.

"Be sure to practice this afternoon, slow and simple, many scales," she said as I was leaving. I had pinned the message back in my hair. "The Lord above knows what sleeping in a haystack has done to your vocal cords."

⌒

At home Maman and Papa were having breakfast. Maman had been only slightly concerned by my absence. "The buses weren't running right," I said. "We got back so late that I stayed with Madame Marcelle."

Papa kissed the top of my head as he went out. I flinched, afraid the dratted message would crackle. "You should take a bath," he said. "*Hein?* Her sofa must be damp—you smell so musty."

Chapter Eighteen

$\mathcal{I}$ had to find a safer place to hide the messages. Sitting in the warm bath, I had an inspiration. I stretched out my wet arm and picked up one of my shoes. Maman had managed to buy them for me only six months before, and they were fine stylish shoes, with high, thick Cuban heels. They weren't as well made as shoes before the war, but I was very proud of them.

Now I tugged at the smooth piece of leather covering the insole. It peeled up, revealing the bottom of the shoe and the wooden base of the heel. The heel was solid, as I had hoped it would be. There would be a way.

After I had bathed and dressed I went out to the back garden, to the shed where my father kept some tools. I found a hand drill and took it to my room.

"What are you doing, Suzanne?" Maman called from the kitchen as I went up the stairs.

"Nothing, Maman," I said. I went into my room and closed the door. It took me some time to figure out how to work the drill, but finally, with the shoe clamped upright between my knees, I managed to carve a hole through the top of the heel. I blew the sawdust away and examined it. When I pulled the leather insole down, it hid the hole completely. I took the message out of my bathrobe pocket, tucked it into the hole, covered the hole with the insole, and buckled the shoe onto my foot. I stood up and walked around. The shoe felt just the same. It was a good hiding place. Anyone who noticed that the insole was loose would not think anything of it. So many things were hard to get now. Everyone wore ragged shoes.

A week after we finished *The Barber of Seville* the director of the opera company called a meeting to discuss our next performance, which was to be *Rigoletto*. I took a seat in the front of the theater, hugging my elbows from excitement. I loved *Rigoletto*.

The director cleared his throat and waited until he had everyone's attention. "First, the bad news," he said. "With the spring rains it becomes ever more obvious that we can no longer wait to repair the roof." This was true—some of the seats in the theater had buckets on them, and now and again, even when it wasn't raining, we could hear a *ping!* from a drop coming through the ceiling. "Therefore," the director continued, "we will be unable to sing in Cherbourg this spring."

Some of the company around me groaned, but I held very still. Not sing! What would I do if I couldn't sing? How would I sleep at all without the lullaby strains of the opera I was learning running through my head?

"The good news," the director said, "is that we have been able to secure another house for two performances." He smiled. "We will perform *Rigoletto* at the Palais Garnier in Paris."

Paris! I clutched my chest. Paris, where the famed national company put on some of the best opera in the world. I would be singing in Paris!

〜ᴧ

I won the lead of Gilda for *Rigoletto*. I practiced as I had never practiced before. "This part is so difficult for a girl your age," Madame Marcelle fretted. "You must take care, Suzanne. Go easy on yourself. If you miss a note, it's not the end of the world. It will be worse if you strain your voice."

"Madame," I said, "I am singing in *Paris.* I can't miss a note."

"It is not the national opera company you are singing with. It is the same Cherbourg company as always." My teacher smiled at me. I knew she understood. I might be singing with the Cherbourg company, but most of the audience would be from Paris. Surely the national director would come. Perhaps I could impress him. Perhaps, after the war, he would send for me. I would sing all across Europe after the war. *Rigoletto* would be my first Parisian performance, but I vowed it would not be my last.

Meanwhile, I suddenly had more messages to deliver than ever. From one or two messages each week I now had one each day, sometimes more, every single day without respite. I hid them in my hollow shoe; I cut slits in the shoulder pads of my dresses and slid them inside. Still, there remained that point of transfer, when I held the paper in my hand. That was the most dangerous time. I grew to dread it. Day after day the doctor sent me out. I ran out of excuses to visit his office, so I stopped making excuses. I disappeared from home and came back hours later.

"More practice?" Maman would ask.

"Oh, yes!" I always said.

"How's it going?"

"Wonderful!"

My number was twenty-two. All along I had never met a person whose number was higher than mine, so I had assumed there were still only twenty-two of us in Cherbourg. Now I began to feel that there were fewer of us remaining. From the start I had made a point of not looking too carefully at any of the other spies. I collected vague impressions of hats, wigs, voices, but I was careful not to pay much attention. I didn't want to be able to identify anyone.

But after I had heard that Monsieur Ventreaux was missing, I had never been sent to meet number four again. For a long time I had met number sixteen, a woman, every month; I no longer did. I had not met Seven in ages, nor Thirteen, nor Twenty. Were they still alive?

Out of fear I began to disguise myself a little. Sometimes I wore my own too-small coat, sometimes Maman's large red one. Sometimes I wore a wide black hat or tied a scarf over my hair. Once I put my hair in pigtails.

I didn't sleep at night. I lay awake and imagined German voices, harsh and loud, the steps of German soldiers thundering up the stairs. I imagined being dragged from my bed, Maman screaming. . . . When I did sleep, I woke drenched in sweat, shaking from the force of my nightmares. It was a miracle I could sing. My old prayer, *Make me strong,* no longer seemed to have any power. Only singing kept me steady. Singing kept me strong.

"I can't keep manufacturing excuses for you," Madame Marcelle told me crossly. "You do too much. You put yourself at risk each day."

I turned my back to her and looked out the window of her apartment. A German soldier patrolled the street below. "I can't stop," I said. "Something must be happening, *madame,* to create so much work for me to do. Something good. The in—"

She put up her hand. I stopped, cutting off the word *invasion.* I was grateful there was anyone at all in this world I could confide in. I didn't want to burden Madame Marcelle too much.

The invasion was what we prayed for: the invasion of France by the Allies. We knew that American soldiers were in England now. Our German-controlled news agencies would never say so, but the British broadcast the truth, and enough French people still had hidden radios that word got out. To conquer Hitler, the Allies would have to attack German-occupied Europe. Where else to do it, I thought, but France? The beaches of Normandy, the beaches near Cherbourg, were the closest mainland Europe came to England. The English Channel was treacherous, the tides were tricky, and the German army was so strong that on one hand an invasion didn't seem possible. On the other hand, it came to seem inevitable. I carried more messages every day. There had to be a purpose behind them.

I didn't question Dr. Leclerc. His face had grown haggard; he seemed as worn and thin as an old piece of paper. I couldn't bear to trouble him. One day when I went to his office, he was holding his small son on his lap. He cradled him with great tenderness. He looked up at me and smiled. "My dear?" he said politely in a questioning tone, as though he hadn't sent for me himself.

"I'm going to Paris on Thursday," I said. "I'll be back late Sunday night."

Dr. Leclerc smiled again—a little sadly, I thought. "I've heard," he said. "I wish I could go to hear you sing."

"All my family will be there," I said. "Madame Marcelle as well. Papa has got train tickets for us all." This was one of the great advantages of Papa's job—when we needed to, we could travel, even in wartime.

"I know a lovely restaurant in Paris, not far from the opera house," he said. "My wife and I dined there on our honeymoon. Perhaps you might enjoy it." He shifted his son more firmly onto his lap and reached into the desk drawer for some paper. He wrote down the name of the restaurant, folded the paper, and slid it into an envelope. His boy watched everything quietly.

"Here you are, then," he said. "Good luck, Suzanne. Good luck in Paris. But hurry home. We'll miss you."

I took the envelope and left. I knew it would contain a message and my directions, as well as the note about the restaurant. The sooner I got the message into my shoe the better. In the doorway I paused and looked back. Dr. Leclerc still sat in his desk chair, staring at nothing. His boy laid his head against his father's chest, and Dr. Leclerc reached up and stroked the child's hair. I could hardly bear to watch them, and yet I stood for a minute or more before I walked away.

CHAPTER NINETEEN

*P*aris, oh, Paris was wonderful. The streets of the city seemed so white and clean, the buildings so beautiful. Were it not for the swastikas and the Nazi soldiers everywhere, and the lack of decent food, and the general absence of gaiety, you wouldn't know you were in a war. When I said so, Papa spat into the street. "Which only proves you can no longer remember how it was before the war," he said.

"Oh, Papa," Maman scolded. "She has a right to be excited."

Pierre tucked his hand into mine. "She's our little opera star. Our artist."

"Our tiny singer," Etienne said, "with such a huge voice."

"Such a loud mouth," said Pierre.

"Such a big head."

They were teasing, but they were proud of me, I knew. Everyone was proud of me. Gilda was a challenging part for an experienced singer, which, as Madame Marcelle took pains to remind me, I was not. Yet I could do it. In rehearsals I hit every note, and my voice was still strong at the end.

Both my uncles came to the first performance. The house was packed, with far larger crowds than we ever had in Cherbourg. As I waited in the wings for the bars of my entrance, my heart beat as fast as it ever had when I was working as a spy. This was it, my big chance. This was Paris. I danced onto the stage proudly, my head held high. I was someone to be noticed. I sang as well as I ever had before.

But Madame Marcelle proved right in her worrying. There is a section in *Rigoletto* where Gilda's part goes very, very high, nearly to the limits of the human voice. All along I had had to stretch just a little to find the uppermost note. As I reached for it during the second of our two performances, I felt something in my throat give—a little, just a little. It wasn't exactly painful, and I could continue to sing. I was glad the high part was over. I didn't think I could hit that note again.

I finished. I made my bow in triumph before a standing ovation. The manager of the theater piled roses into my arms.

The next morning I couldn't speak. My throat felt wounded. Any noise I made came out as a croak.

"Don't say a word," Madame Marcelle said grimly. "You must not make the damage worse."

"Mon Dieu," Maman said, pressing her hands against the sides of my neck. "Oh, Suzanne, don't cry. When we get home we'll take you to the doctor."

I thought of Dr. Leclerc and the messages that surely awaited me. I rubbed my hand against my throat. At least now, I thought, I wouldn't need an excuse to see him.

The train home was crowded with German soldiers. I pressed my head against the smooth window glass and tried to sleep. I knew that losing my voice had nothing to do with the war, but I felt that everything bad was pressing upon me at once. Singing gave me something else besides spying to think about, something else to do. The first night home from Paris I woke three times from hideous nightmares, shaking and bathed in sweat. Maman didn't come to me, so I guessed I had not cried out. After the last nightmare I was too tense to sleep again. I watched the gray walls of my bedroom and tried not to think of Hitler, of the death camps my Parisian uncles had talked about, of the fate that stalked me.

First thing next morning Dr. Leclerc's daughter came to the door. "Papa wants to see Suzanne," I heard her say. I was still in bed. I had dozed off sometime after dawn.

"*Sacré bleu,*" Maman said. "Good heavens! Has he heard about her poor voice already?"

I got up and threw on a dress and went downstairs. "My darling," Maman said, "have some tea before you run off. It will soothe your throat."

I sat at the table. The tea she gave me had sugar in it, despite how precious sugar had become. It did go down easily.

"You look horrible," said Etienne.

I grabbed a pencil and scribbled on a scrap of paper, "I couldn't sleep."

Etienne patted my hand. "Don't worry. Voices can heal. Better than broken backs, I should think."

Could they? Well enough to sing opera? I didn't know. I couldn't speak above a whisper. It frightened me, though not as much as the idea of relaying a message that day. I looked at Etienne and his crutches, and I felt ashamed. Yet I wasn't ready to be a spy again, not after such a night. *You can never back out,* I reminded myself. *Once you begin, you cannot stop. And you did begin.*

⌒⌄

Dr. Leclerc looked down my throat with a little penlight. He shook his head. "You've strained your vocal cords badly, I fear," he said. "But as you know, this is not my area of expertise. It would be better if you saw a specialist."

I took a pad of paper and wrote, "Where can I go to a specialist?"

He shook his head. "It would be better, Suzanne, but it may not be possible. I don't know. Perhaps in Paris. If you don't begin to improve in a few weeks, I will make inquiries. It's all so difficult right now."

A few weeks!

"You must not scream or shout or attempt to sing," he said. "You must speak as little and as quietly as possible. You must gargle with salt water four times a day. I will want to see you every morning." He didn't acknowledge how convenient this would be for the messages. We were alone in his office, and he continued in the same calm voice, "I have three messages for you today."

"Three!" It came out in a hoarse whisper.

"I mean it about not trying to shout," he said. "Yes, three. It will be a busy week. We are all glad you are back. We need you."

CHAPTER TWENTY

*M*onday, three messages. Tuesday, three messages. Wednesday, six messages—six! I crisscrossed the city. I knew I was becoming conspicuous. I was in more strange places at strange hours than I should be. I had begun to recognize some of the German officers on the street as individuals, not just faceless soldiers. My small attempts at disguise seemed so obvious and useless that I gave them up; I feared I was looking too much as though I had something to hide.

But if I could recognize German officers, when would they be able to recognize me?

Thursday, four messages.

By Friday I still couldn't speak above a whisper. Madame Marcelle wept over my voice. She made me tea and told me to gargle very conscientiously indeed. "We will not think of your singing now," she said. "All our thoughts will be about singing later. You must be diligent."

I would be diligent. When the war was over, I would be famous—or so I told myself, to get through each day.

"I have to go," I whispered.

"Stay," she said. "I've borrowed a new recording of *La Bohème*. I want to play it for you."

"I have to go," I repeated. "I have to . . ." I let my words trail off. Madame Marcelle would understand. But she stared at me as if she didn't. "It's a busy time," I said. I had only stopped at Madame Marcelle's to give myself an excuse to walk that way. I had six messages. Too many. I had barely slept all week.

"Last night—" Madame Marcelle began. She stopped and looked at me for a long moment. "Last night I heard something on the radio. On the BBC."

I sucked in my breath. The BBC was the British Broadcasting Corporation, the radio service from England. "Are you a spy?" I whispered.

She shook her head. "I know someone with a radio, that's all," she said. "Sometimes I listen to it. No, my dear. The only spy I know is you." She smiled. "But last night the BBC read part of a French poem by Paul Verlaine. 'Chanson d'Automne.' Do you know it?" She recited a few words.

"I don't know it," I said. "I don't know why they read it. I don't know what it means."

"There are signals, you know, all the time," Madame Marcelle said. "On the radio. This poem—it was in French, not translated, and they read only the first three lines."

I put my hat on. I was impatient to be gone. Already I might be keeping number eighteen waiting, putting him in danger. I had met Eighteen seven times that week. I had only met a total of five other spies. I didn't like to think about what that implied. "I don't know what it means," I said. "I don't know anything, *madame*, except where to go and whom to meet when I get there. The messages are all in code."

Madame Marcelle paused in front of the door. "I'll tell you if they broadcast the rest of the poem," she said. "I asked my friend to let me know."

"Thank you," I said. I went out without looking back. I was simply not interested. What did it matter if signals were being sent via the BBC? I knew something would happen soon. It had to. Dr. Leclerc wouldn't send me out so often and ask me to be so obvious if it were in any way possible for him to delay.

⌒ᴧ

Saturday night I lay awake on my bed, weeping. I was so tired that my hands trembled. I feared sleep. I knew the dreams that awaited me. I didn't want to dream them again.

That very day Maman had measured me for a new summer dress. She had found a piece of linen somewhere, and though I didn't really like the color, it was better than anything I had had in a long time. Maman slipped her tape around my waist, then drew back, startled. "Suzanne! You have lost weight!" She measured my hips and bust. Her eyes darkened. "Just since I made the costumes for *Rigoletto,* only a month ago. A girl like you shouldn't lose weight. You must eat. I don't care if you are worried about your voice. You must stay strong."

Part of me wanted to fall apart right then, to put my arms around my strong mother and tell her everything. I knew better, of course. "Oh, Maman, I eat plenty," I whispered. "You know I do. I even eat the horrible rutabagas. I'm not pining away."

"Are you sick?" She searched my face. "Do you feel ill at all?"

"I haven't slept very well since *Rigoletto,*" I said. "But I'm trying, Maman. I don't know why I would lose weight. I feel fine. I promise."

"This voice of yours—"

"It's a little better, I think. The saltwater treatments help. I'll be fine."

Maman kissed me. "Yes, my strong daughter. I'm sure you will be."

I was worried about my voice. When I let myself think about it, I felt panicked. I couldn't imagine a world in which I didn't sing. But although I gargled four times a day, in between I didn't let myself think about singing. I had too much else to think about, too many messages to carry. The effort of appearing innocent took all my strength.

Sunday I couldn't go to church. Papa threw a fit. "No child of mine pretends to be an invalid!" he roared, waving his fists inside the doorway of my room. "You will get out of that bed and you will go!"

"I don't feel well," I said without moving. "I need to stay home."

"Oh, let her stay," pleaded Maman. "She's worn out."

"No one is too worn out for church," Papa said. "There is no such thing. Do you have a fever?" He came into the room and put his hand on my forehead.

"I think I have to use the toilet—often. Too often," I said. "I'll never be able to sit through Mass. Papa—"

Papa wrinkled his nose. I wasn't sure he believed me. Why should he, such a lie? I hadn't used the toilet all morning. "Well!" he said, throwing up his hands. "Stay where you are. Sleep the Sabbath away. The sin will be on your conscience, not mine." He stomped down the stairs. "Come, boys, your sister lies in bed this morning."

I waited ten minutes after they had gone, until I was

certain that Mass must have started. Then I dressed quickly and dashed from the house. Dr. Leclerc had met me late the night before on his way home from delivering a baby; "Between nine and ten A.M.," he had said. Which was fine except that church began at nine. Still, if I was quick, I would be back in bed before my family came home.

After Mass Aunt Suzanne came with her battalion. I got out of bed as soon as they all returned. "Oh, I feel much better now," I said carelessly. "It must have been something I ate."

"Bah," Papa said. "The rest of us aren't sick. You ate nothing except what we ate."

"At Madame Marcelle's, maybe. I must go see her this afternoon."

Could I pass this off? I had always been good. I had always done what I was told. I had never behaved as I was behaving now.

"Suzanne!" Maman reproached me. "On a Sunday, with your cousins here?"

"I promised, Maman. She—she is not feeling well." Oh, the lies became clumsier now that there were so many of them. I had to be in a hotel lobby at two o'clock. After that I was to go down to the quay.

"You will not go out of this house today," Papa said sternly. "If you are too sick to go to church, you are too sick to go to Madame Marcelle's." To my aunt he said,

"She runs wild these days. Ever since we came back from Paris."

"Poor dear," Aunt Suzanne said sympathetically. "It must be so hard, injuring your voice."

I did not say anything. I tried to be useful in the kitchen. At one-thirty, just before everyone sat down to dinner, I left the house. I walked away quickly, praying hard that Maman or Papa would not come after me.

After the meeting in the lobby I had another message, and another. It was six o'clock before I got home. Aunt Suzanne and my cousins had gone.

"You're going to catch it now," Pierre said as I walked up the steps.

I did not stop walking or even slow down. My parents got up from their chairs as I passed them. Papa began to yell and wave his arms. I couldn't hear him. It wasn't that I wasn't listening; I was truly too worn out to make sense of what he said. I went straight up the stairs to my room. I lay flat on my bed and fell asleep instantly. For once I didn't dream.

CHAPTER TWENTY-ONE

On Monday morning at the breakfast table Papa had plenty left to say, and this time I heard it all. I was an ungrateful daughter. I was acting like a fool. I was gone too much, I was rude, I disobeyed. Why was I behaving this way? What were my reasons?

"Yes, Papa," I whispered. My voice hurt.

Who did I think I was, to show such disrespect to my mother, to my aunt? Why?

I was a spy.

"I'm sorry, Papa." I did not offer excuses. I had none that could be believed. My brothers sat silent, staring at their plates. Maman looked unhappy. Papa went on and on.

"Well," he said at last, picking up his fork, "I can tell you one thing. You're not going anywhere today, not if I have to tie you to a chair."

I cleared my throat and tried to swallow a sip of tea.

"But I'm getting my hair cut," I whispered. "I have an appointment." When Papa said nothing I added, "Madame Marcelle said she would come with me. She wants to show the hairdresser a new style."

This, thank heaven, was the absolute truth. I could not fake getting my hair cut. And Madame Marcelle *did* want to come with me. Never mind the message I had to deliver first, or the ones I felt were sure to come afterward. Once I was out of the house, I didn't have to come back.

"No," Papa said, "No haircut." He laid his hands flat on the table. The cat purred around his ankles, but for once Papa ignored Miki. "You are not to leave the house."

"Papa," I said, "I've had this appointment for two weeks."

"No," he said.

I nodded. "Very well." I was pretty sure he wouldn't tie me to a chair. At the worst he would shut me in my room—and the room had a window, and the window opened.

You can't tell anyone. Not your mother, not your brothers, not your best friend. And if you agree to help me, you can never back out. I couldn't stop. I wouldn't.

"She should go," Maman said quietly.

"What's this?"

"Let her get her hair cut, Papa," Maman said. "This is a hard time. Let her be happy about a new haircut."

"Bah," said Papa.

"She's a good girl," Maman said. "Let her go."

Miki meowed. Papa bent to pick the cat up. "All right, then," he said. "Get your hair cut. But then you come straight home."

"Yes, Papa," I said.

Maman patted my hand. "We know how upset you are about your voice," she said. "Don't worry. It'll come back."

◠〜

I delivered the message before I went to Madame Marcelle's. I gave it to number ten, a woman I recognized easily despite the fact that she was wearing a wig. I had met her twice only the day before. *Twice.* Lord in heaven, were there so few of us left? Fear clung to her like a bad smell.

"Is it so bad?" Madame Marcelle asked me when she opened her door.

"Oh, how do I know? I think it is."

"Well." Madame Marcelle set her hat upon her head. "We will get your hair cut anyhow."

We walked down the street to the shop where I always got my hair cut. The woman who owned it sometimes gave me a special set just before my performances. When we walked in, she smiled at me, an extra-large, how-wonderful-to-see-you smile. "Suzanne," she said. "How lovely. I wasn't sure you would come in today."

"Madame Marcelle has a picture to show you," I said. I settled myself into the chair.

"I think it would look good onstage," Madame Marcelle said. She took it out of her purse.

The hairdresser waved her fingers at us. "Certainly, certainly, excellent," she said. "Just let me make one little phone call and I'll be right with you."

I leaned back into the soft cushioned chair. This woman always washed my hair before she cut it, and I loved the feeling of her fingernails against my scalp. That and the warm water would feel especially nice today, when I was so tense.

The hairdresser came back into the front room. She put a towel around my neck and fastened it in back. Then she bent over the picture Madame Marcelle showed her. I closed my eyes.

The door of the shop slammed open. Madame Marcelle screamed. I jumped up, nearly knocking over the chair. A group of German soldiers burst into the shop. Six of them—one was an officer. They raised their guns and pointed them at me.

The officer pulled me toward him. Madame Marcelle clung to me, but he pushed her away. He yanked the towel from my neck and shoved me toward the soldiers. Two of them grabbed my hands. They pulled my arms behind my back and bound them together with something strong. *"Madame!"* I shrieked.

"Suzanne!" She looked at me in despair. "I don't understand! I don't understand at all!"

The soldiers must have thought she meant she knew nothing, for they left her alone. But I knew she meant she had done nothing, she had not betrayed me.

"I know," I said. "I know."

The hairdresser put her arm around the Nazi officer and laid her cheek against his chest.

"I'm sorry, Suzanne," she said in a soft, throaty voice. She lifted her chin, and the officer kissed her. "But you see, I support a different cause."

So that was the phone call she had made—a call to her Nazi lover to say I was there. But how had they known about me in the first place? It couldn't have been solely the hairdresser's fault.

It didn't matter. I was caught. The soldiers marched me at gunpoint through the cobblestone streets in the full light of early morning. I did not cry out to any of the people we passed, but neither did I look away from them. I held my head high and nodded to everyone I recognized. *If this is the end, let them remember that I went with dignity,* I thought. *Dear God, make me strong.*

Chapter Twenty-two

They took me to the city jail, which the Germans had commandeered at the start of the occupation. They unshackled my hands and took me to a small room, where they sat me on a hard wooden chair. There was one light, no window. Across the room were a table and a few comfortable chairs, where the Germans sat while they pointed their guns at me.

You must just hold on, I told myself. There wouldn't have been so many messages in so few days without a reason. Something would happen soon. *You must hold on,* I thought, *as long as ever you can. You must be strong.*

A more important-looking Nazi came into the room with a stack of papers in his hand. He sat at the table and pulled out a pen.

"What is your name?" he asked in heavily accented French.

"Suzanne David."

"Do you know why we have you here?"

I thanked Mary and all the saints above that I didn't have a message on my person. "No."

"We think you are a spy."

It wasn't a question, so I didn't reply.

"We are sure you are a spy."

It was hot in the room. There was no breeze.

"Are you a spy?"

"No." I wasn't going to say anything more than the minimum.

"We are going to kill you, of course," said the officer. "But maybe not if you give us the answers we need."

I thought suddenly of a fable we had learned in school. A fox made a deal with a scorpion to carry the scorpion on its back across a river. Halfway over, the scorpion stung the fox. "Why did you do that?" cried the fox. "Now we will both drown." The scorpion replied, "It is my nature."

It was the Germans' nature to kill me. Giving them answers would not change a thing.

"Do you know Dr. Stéphane Leclerc?"

Oh, please, no, not the doctor.

"Of course," I said.

"Do you know what he does?"

"Helps deliver babies and cares for the sick."

"And what else?"

"That's all."

"Why do you go to his office so often?"

I put my hand to my throat. "I strained my voice," I said. "I'm a singer. He is trying to heal me."

"Are you a spy?"

"I am an opera singer."

"We are certain that you are a spy."

⌒

So the morning went. About lunchtime I was led from the room and taken to another. There two woman soldiers (female German soldiers! I had never seen any in Cherbourg before) removed my clothing and searched me. They ran their hands through my hair. They gave me another dress to wear and carried off everything I had worn. I wondered if they would find the slits in my shoulder pads, the empty hole in the heel of my shoe.

"May I use the toilet?" I asked the one who seemed to be in charge.

She glared at me and spoke in rapid German to the other, who asked in French, "What did you say?"

I repeated the question. *"Non!"* snapped the second woman without bothering to translate for the first.

I really needed to use a toilet.

They took me back to the first room, to the uncomfortable chair. The guards and the officer were all eating lunch. They had a big meal spread across their table. They had roast beef and wine.

I wasn't hungry. I couldn't have swallowed food if they had demanded it of me. I studied the plaster of the wall behind their heads and tried not to think about anything.

When they were finished and the food was taken away, they resumed their questions.

"Are you a spy?"

"No."

"Do you carry messages for Dr. Leclerc?"

"No."

"We know that you do. We have the names of everyone. Come, confess. It will be easier for you if you do."

Sometimes they tried a different tack. "What's in the messages you pass? Have you tried to read them?"

And later still, lies. "De Gaulle is dead, you know. The Allies have suffered heavy losses. France is lost."

They never hit me or hurt me. They never screamed or shouted. They never let me get up from the chair again and they never stopped questioning me. I knew that moving water could wear away rock, and now I understood how. *But you must be more than a rock,* I told myself. *You must be something that doesn't wear away.*

I was. I didn't cry. I didn't give in. I made my voice

level, soft, so that I would not further harm my vocal cords. In the intervals of silence they granted me, I prayed. *Je vous salue, Marie, pleine de grâce, le Seigneur est avec vous. . . .* Hail Mary, full of grace, the Lord is with you. I would have counted a rosary on my fingers, but the silence never lasted that long. I prayed, *Make me strong.*

I could tell when night fell because the light coming from the hallway changed. The officer left and another took his place.

"You're a silly child to deny the truth," this one said harshly. "What would your mother say? Your father, your two brothers, Etienne and Pierre? Hmmm? I wonder what they will say tomorrow morning when we knock on their door. Perhaps they are all spies too."

If I had broken down, it would have been then, when I thought of Maman being captured by these cretins. "Papa was in the cavalry," I said. "He served under de Gaulle." Please heaven, he would understand. He would not remember his daughter as a fool.

Hold on, I told myself. *Hold on as long as you can.*

A guard brought this officer supper, steaming potatoes and a mound of sliced beef. It looked as though it had been cut from the same roast that the other officer had eaten for lunch. It was warm and had gravy poured onto it, and the potatoes were covered with gravy too. By now my stomach was complaining despite my fear.

It had been a long time since I had eaten good roast beef, and the gravy smelled so good that I longed for a taste. The officer seemed to sense this. He held up each forkful for me to see, and he smacked his lips and chewed with gusto. He washed it all down with a glass of red wine. Then he sent for a pitcher of water and a fresh glass. He poured a glass of water.

"Thirsty, Suzanne?" he asked.

"Yes, please," I said.

"Ah, too bad." He drank the water, then had the glass taken away. "Now. Why don't you admit that you're a spy? Then you could get some sleep. I'm sure you're tired. It's getting late, you know. Your parents must be worried."

In another part of the building a door must have opened. For a moment I could hear a shout, a confused babble of voices, and something in French that sounded like "I won't go, no! No! You said you would—" Then a door slammed shut, and I couldn't hear any more.

The German officer sighed. He crossed his hands on top of the table. "It's always so much better when people cooperate," he said. "Tell me how you became a spy."

⌒ⱽ

The night passed. The wording of the questions stayed the same, but the tone they were asked in became more insistent, more persuasive. I was too terrified to feel sleepy, but I began to have moments when my brain seemed disconnected from the rest of me. I would see the officer's lips moving and not understand what he asked. Worse, I would find myself in the middle of a sentence and not know what I had just said. I crossed my arms and pinched the soft flesh below my rib cage, hard, to make myself concentrate. I could not give in. I would not give in.

Finally the German officer rose from his chair. He nudged one of the guards, who jumped as though he had been asleep. The officer let loose a torrent of German. The guard hung his head. Both left the room, shutting the door behind them. The other two guards, more alert now, watched me carefully.

The door opened and the first German officer, the one from the morning before, came in. He looked refreshed and clean. He carried a cup of coffee that smelled like heaven. My lips were parched and my dry throat hurt. Of course, I thought, the way I needed to use the toilet, it was lucky they hadn't given me anything to drink. I smiled to myself over that, just a tiny bit.

The officer looked at me. His eyebrows shot to his forehead. "So you find us amusing?" He set his cup upon the table. "You're a tough little girl, I give you that. But you can't win, *mademoiselle*. You see, there is only one of you, and there are a great number of us.

You may as well give in now. You may as well admit the truth."

Hold on, I thought.

Suddenly, somewhere in the building, many doors slammed at once. Voices shouted in German, lots of voices, loud and harsh, more and more urgently. Feet pounded down the corridor. The guards in my room jumped up. The officer, who was about to take a sip of coffee, went rigid with his arm in midair.

I sat very still.

The door to the room flew open. A man I couldn't see yelled something frantic in German. The officer in the room barked a question. The man answered as he ran down the hall. The officer slammed his coffee cup onto the table and ran out, the guards at his heels. Throughout the entire building came a cacophony of pounding feet, shouting voices, slamming doors. Words I couldn't understand washed over me like an angry sea.

I didn't move.

Perhaps three minutes went by. The noises receded until the building became so quiet it seemed empty. Perhaps it was empty. I stood up, very slowly. I walked to the table and took a sip of the German officer's coffee. It was warm and very, very good. But then I thought of the officer drinking it, and I set the cup down.

Still the building was silent. I wondered when the guards would return. I peeked out of the doorway. Down the long hall I could see other doors standing open. I could smell a fresh sea breeze. Where had they gone?

Don't be a fool, I told myself. What did it matter where they had gone? They were gone. I squared my shoulders and began to walk down the hall.

I was almost to the main entrance when a man stepped out of another room. I jumped and screamed.

He looked dazed. "Are they really gone?" he asked in French.

I looked at him. He was dressed like a French civilian, not a German soldier. "I think so," I said. "I don't know why."

The man smiled, but his eyes remained troubled. "Surely you can guess," he said.

"I can guess. I just don't believe it."

He nodded. "Well. No use standing here, eh?" We stepped outside. The morning light was blinding. "Who are you?" he asked me. "I should know, shouldn't I?"

"What do you mean?"

He smiled, and suddenly I recognized him. "You," I said, "you're Fourteen."

He said, "You're Twenty-two."

A group of German soldiers ran around the corner

right past us. Fourteen and I flinched. The soldiers jumped into a nearby jeep and roared away without looking at us at all.

Fourteen smiled again. "It's over," he said. "You know that, don't you?"

I nodded. "Yes."

It was Tuesday, the sixth of June, 1944. The Allies had invaded the beaches of Normandy and saved me.

CHAPTER TWENTY-THREE

*F*ourteen and I continued to walk down the street. No one seemed to notice us. "I think we're all that's left," he said.

"All that's left?"

"They took the rest," he said. "Last night a busload of prisoners went to Saint-Lô. I could see the bus leave from the room where they were questioning me. They found out all of our names. We were all caught at the end. Didn't you know?"

I shook my head.

"When I think of what they did to the poor doctor—"

I stopped. "What did they do to the doctor?"

"My child—"

"What did they do to the doctor?"

"They killed him," Fourteen said. "He and his wife and his children. They killed them all."

If I had had anything in my stomach, I would have thrown it up right there. I felt as though a heavy weight had struck me. My breath came in gulps.

"Don't you understand?" Fourteen said. "They will kill the ones they took away. They have killed everyone they captured before. All of us but you and me."

All of us but you and me. Dr. Leclerc. His little boy. Thirteen, who met me in church. Ten, who seemed so afraid. Seven, the old woman with wispy gray hair. Monsieur Ventreaux, who was number four. Everyone but Fourteen and me.

Fourteen turned to go to his home, and I walked down my street, dizzy with exhaustion and grief.

Papa, Maman, Madame Marcelle, Etienne, and Pierre were all clustered in the parlor when I opened the door. Maman and Madame Marcelle were crying, and Papa's eyes were red.

I stood in the doorway, swaying. *"Suzanne!"* Someone grabbed me, pulled me through the doorway. Maman clutched my neck, sobbing. Madame Marcelle clutched my arms, sobbing. The boys shouted, and Papa tried to push us all out of the way so he could shut the door and lock the Germans out.

Everyone spoke at once. "They came and got you—" "Madame Marcelle told us—" "What did they want with you?" "My little one, are you hurt?"—this last a heartfelt cry from Maman.

"I'm not hurt. They didn't touch me," I said.

"But why—"

Etienne gripped my hands. "They came for the doctor."

"I know." I took a deep breath. "I think he might be dead."

"Yes," said Etienne. "They killed him in the street."

Maman began to weep again. "You're all right, you aren't hurt," she sobbed.

"The invasion has started," said Pierre.

"I know that too."

"How?" shouted Papa. "How did you know these things? What did the Nazis want with my daughter?"

I sank onto the sofa. "I'm a spy," I said. "I'm a spy." All the tears I had held back spilled down my cheeks. I covered my face with my hands. "I'm a spy."

"You can't be a spy!" cried Maman. "Suzanne, no! That's ridiculous!"

"You put yourself in danger!" shouted Papa. "My God! My God! What were you thinking?"

Etienne slid next to me. He took my hands and pulled them away from my face. "My little sister," he whispered. "A hero of France."

Papa stopped pacing. "Well, yes," he said. "Yes. My God, she is."

I tried to answer their questions, but I was so tired and overwrought that Maman soon insisted I be allowed to go to bed. She helped me upstairs. When I went in to use the toilet, she brought me a nightgown and made me remove the dress the Nazis had given me. I don't know what she did with it; I never saw it again.

When I woke, it was midafternoon. I lay still for a moment, savoring the heavy relaxed feeling in my arms and legs. I hadn't slept so well in three years. It was because I was no longer afraid.

My part was over. The Allies were landing. The war would end.

I went slowly down the stairs. I could smell the most wonderful smells, roast lamb and garlic and rosemary, and hear the happiest voices, my brothers, my cousins, my aunt. I went into the kitchen. Pierre stood up and began to applaud, and then everyone did—my whole family, Madame Marcelle too. I began to smile.

"Come," said Maman. She led me into the dining room. The table had been set with the nicest dishes we still had. In the center was a huge bowl of fresh flowers, and in front of that was a cake with white icing. Cake! I had not tasted cake in years.

My cousins crowded around the table. "Look, Suzanne!" they cried. "With sugar! It's sweet!"

Papa took out a bottle and carefully pulled its cork. Bubbles frothed. Papa laughed. He poured a glass and handed it to me. I took a sip, and everyone cheered. It was my very first taste of champagne.

We ate the cake first and afterward Maman served roast lamb and the flageolets I loved so well. "Your brothers bought everything," Maman said. "Lord knows where they found that cake. They have been out most of the day."

"The Allies are landing on the beaches twenty kilometers from here," said Pierre. "All the Germans have rushed there. I didn't see any in town."

I nodded. "They questioned me all night," I said. "In the morning they started shouting, and they ran out. When I realized they were gone, I left."

"What did you tell them?" Papa asked.

"Nothing," I said. "Not one word." *I am strong.*

He looked proud. "Well done," he said. "Who knows, perhaps someday even General de Gaulle will hear what you did."

"Papa." A strange sense of triumph rose in me. "Papa, he already knows."

The room went quiet. Papa put down his glass and stared at me. "General de Gaulle knows who I am," I said. "He has my photograph. He knows all about me."

Into the astonished silence I continued, "It was real, Papa. What I did was real. I've been a spy for three years. I was a good one. None of you knew. The Germans didn't know. But General de Gaulle knew, because Dr. Leclerc told him. And the Allies landing here, now—part of that is because of me. Because of the messages I carried. Because of all of us, what we did."

Pierre said, "But you just don't look like a spy."

I couldn't help laughing. "A spy who looks like a spy wouldn't last long. You should have believed me, Pierre. I'm a better actress than you guessed. I've been an artist all along."

EPILOGUE

$\mathcal{T}$he messages I carried gave the details of landing places, tides and currents, German forces, bridges, and cities that the Allies needed to know to plan the D-Day invasion. I learned this later, when the war was over.

On June 22, two weeks after D-Day, the Allies began their attack on Cherbourg. The Germans had fallen back to defend the city; because of its ammunition stores and submarine facilities, Hitler had ordered it held to the last round. Allied air forces dropped a thousand tons of bombs on Cherbourg in the final two hours, most aimed directly at the submarine bunkers. None fell near my home, though you may be sure we huddled downstairs away from the windows that day. I can still hear the noise of those bombs in my head.

Five days later the Allies liberated Cherbourg. The Germans, what was left of them, were lined up in long rows on the beaches at the harbor, loaded onto prison ships, and carried away.

In September I received the Croix de Lorraine in Paris from General Charles de Gaulle himself. The Croix was a medal given to those who fought in the Resistance. De Gaulle shook my hand, bowed his head, and said, "Thank you, *mademoiselle,* for all you have done." I couldn't help thinking of the others, the twenty spies in Cherbourg who didn't live to be so honored.

We discovered that Dr. Leclerc had had a secret room in his basement, where he kept a radio transmitter that he used to communicate directly with the Allies in England. Radio transmissions were frighteningly easy to intercept; Dr. Leclerc had been very clever to remain undetected for so long.

Madame Marcelle took a job in Italy after the end of the war. She died a few years later without my having seen her again. As far as I know, Yvette did not recover.

The hairdresser who had betrayed me stood trial after I left France. Papa wrote that she walked like an old woman, frail and bent, when she took the stand. She was found guilty of consorting with the enemy and sent to prison. But before that she was herded into the street and every hair on her head was shaved off. That was how they treated German sympathizers after the war.

I left France to go to America, to join my husband,

an American soldier named Larson Hall. We fell in love when his regiment was stationed in Cherbourg; we were married in the Church of La Trinité on December 21, 1945. Larson's home was in Kingsport, Tennessee, a small town surrounded by green hills, far from the ocean I was used to. There was no opera there, nor anyplace for a classically trained singer. So I didn't remain one. I never found out whether my voice would have fully healed. After *Rigoletto* I never performed again.

I sang to my children when they were small. We had a son first, and many years later a daughter. Now we have four grandchildren.

For many years I tried to forget the things that happened to me in the war, but now I find I want to remember. I want the children to know that their grandmother was once saluted by de Gaulle. I want them to know who de Gaulle was and why he mattered. I want them to understand why all of us who were part of the French Resistance risked our lives.

We did it to fight Hitler, of course, and all the evil that he spread. We did it to save innocents; we did it because there were people we could not save. We did it for France, for the way our lives had been before the war. But mostly we did it for ourselves, so that we would never have to look back and admit that we had not acted against the horrors that swirled around us.

We did it for freedom. Our own.

About the Author

KIMBERLY BRUBAKER BRADLEY was born in Fort Wayne, Indiana. After earning her bachelor's degree from Smith College, she worked as a research chemist, then became a freelance writer. Her first novel, *Ruthie's Gift,* won her a *Publishers Weekly* "Flying Start" honor. Her most recent novel was *Halfway to the Sky*. Kimberly Brubaker Bradley and her husband, Bart, have two young children, Matthew and Katie. They live on a farm in eastern Tennessee, in the foothills of the Appalachian Mountains.